Acclaim for S[...]
BIMBOS OF [...]

"*Bimbos* . . . should become a classic instantly."
—*Mystery Scene*

"A hilarious spoof . . . McCrumb is a genuinely funny writer."
—*Toronto Globe and Mail*

"*Bimbos of the Death Sun* lampoons the world of science fiction fans with an over-the-top look at murder at a science fiction convention. . . . One of the funniest pieces of fiction to hit the stands since Elizabeth Peters tackled the romance world in the 1980s."
—KRISTINE KATHRYN RUSCH

"Ms. McCrumb writes with quiet fire and maybe a little mountain magic. Like every storyteller, she has the Sight."
—*The New York Times Book Review*

"In *Bimbos of the Death Sun*, Sharyn McCrumb prove(s) herself to be a master of piercing satire."
—JOAN HESS

*Please turn the page
for more reviews . . .*

"Describing Sharyn McCrumb's wit as sardonic is a bit like describing Saddam Hussein as a guy you wouldn't want to take home to mother. In fact, McCrumb's irreverent sense of humor is as dry as a desert wind and often as lethal as a drifting cloud of mustard gas. . . . She's Agatha Christie with an attitude; outrageous and engrossing at the same time."
—*Nashville Banner*

"For Sharyn McCrumb, just telling a riveting tale of intrigue is not enough. Her books transcend the boundaries of a good read."
—Nikki Giovanni

"(McCrumb) handles drama and comedy with equal ease."
—*San Diego Union-Tribune*

"McCrumb's ability to write in a variety of styles—crossing genres, mixing the comic with the serious—makes her one of the most versatile crime authors on the contemporary scene."
—*Booklist*

"Sharyn McCrumb is definitely a star in the New Golden Age of mystery fiction. I look forward to reading her for a long time to come."
—Elizabeth Peters

"Only a writer as accomplished as Sharyn McCrumb can so skillfully marry farce and tragedy with such rewarding results."
—*The Gainesville Sun*

By Sharyn McCrumb

The Elizabeth MacPherson Novels
(in chronological order)

Published by The Ballantine Publishing Group

BIMBOS OF THE DEATH SUN

Sharyn McCrumb

BALLANTINE BOOKS • NEW YORK

Copyright © 1988 by Sharyn McCrumb
Introduction copyright © 1997 by Sharyn McCrumb

All rights reserved under International and Pan-American Copyright Conventions. Published in the United States by Ballantine Books, a division of Random House, Inc., New York, and distributed in Canada by Random House of Canada Limited, Toronto. Originally published by TSR, Inc. in 1988.

All characters in this book are fictitious. Any resemblance to actual persons, living or dead, is purely coincidental.

http://www.randomhouse.com

Library of Congress Catalog Card Number: 96-97041

ISBN 0-345-41215-X

Manufactured in the United States of America

First Ballantine Books Edition: February 1997

10 9 8 7 6 5 4 3 2

97-1025

AUTHOR'S NOTE

MORE THAN TEN years ago, when I was a struggling graduate student in the Virginia Tech English department, the university science fiction club sponsored a short story contest, to be judged by a colleague of mine, English instructor John Nizalowski. As a practical joke, I slipped an outrageous manuscript into the pile of story entries and waited to hear John's scream when he read it. The spoof was entitled "Bimbos of the Death Sun."

When John had recovered from reading a manuscript in which his dog and his officemate were depicted as evil aliens in a parody of *Moby-Dick*, he returned it to me, saying, "You know, that title is really too good to waste on a practical joke."

"I know," I said. "But I could never write the book that went with that title."

I tucked the idea away in a few spare brain cells in the math section of my cortex and went back to writing the Elizabeth MacPherson novels, which were "Jane Austen with an attitude"—definitely not science fiction.

A few months later, I had an idea that fit the title. What if one of the university's engineering professors wrote a hard science fiction novel about the effect of alien sunspots on computer circuits, and what if he sold that novel to a cheap paperback house, and they changed the title to *Bimbos of the Death Sun*? I pictured the professor going to a small regional SF convention to promote his book and trying to keep his students from finding out that he was the author of the paperback with the lurid bikini-clad girl on the cover. *That* book I could write, I thought.

I completed the first two chapters for fun, drawing on a local science fiction convention called Mysticon for inspiration—and on my observation of my husband's war-gaming friends. Writing those chapters was cheaper than therapy. Still, this wasn't the sort of book that I was writing for my New York editor, Joe Blades, so I put the pages in a drawer and went back to writing term papers on the Brontës and chronicling the adventures of Elizabeth MacPherson.

Then the science fiction club had its own convention. It was being held one weekend at the Blacksburg Econo-Lodge, and the club had raised enough money to bring one—*one*—author in to star in about eight hours of programming. Even as out of touch with reality as they were, they realized that this poor author would need to be given a recess every now and then, so they cast about for other ways to fill the day.

One of them hunted me up on campus. "You! You're a published writer!" he said accusingly.

"Well . . . not anything you guys read," I murmured.

"Doesn't matter. The real author will have to eat,

and so on. Why don't you come and do a one-hour session? A reading, maybe."

I didn't get many offers to give readings in those days, so I accepted the invitation, but I knew the science fiction club wouldn't care for my usual work. Then I remembered those ten pages of *Bimbos of the Death Sun*. I dug them out of the file cabinet and took them to the Econo-Lodge.

The guest author stayed for the reading, laughed harder than anybody, and asked for a copy of the manuscript. I photocopied the pages for her, thinking that she wanted to pass them around the office when she got home. She did—but the office was that of her publisher.

Six months later, I received a phone call at work from a strange man who said, "We want to buy your book."

I said, "What book?"

The rest is history. I agreed to write the rest of the novel in fewer than eight weeks, so my memory of that autumn is a blur of computer screen and exhaustion, but I did finish it. *Bimbos of the Death Sun* was published in the spring of 1987, and it went on to win the Edgar Award that year for Best Paperback Original Mystery. That's when I realized that the joke was on me. I had envisioned a professor haunted by his paperback with its garish cover—and that is exactly what my novel looked like. My cover was *his* cover, and for a long time I would be known as the author of *Bimbos of the Death Sun*. Try living that down!

Then the book proceeded to have a life of its own. At book signings in Hollywood, cast members of science fiction television programs turned up with battered copies of *Bimbos of the Death Sun*. "We use it as a survival manual," one of them told me. "It's the best way to explain to guest stars what they'll experience when they go to a fan convention."

SF fandom discovered the book, and readers either loved it or were outraged by the description of fandom. Panel discussions debated the issues raised in the novel. I felt like the Salman Rushdie of science fiction. People from all over the U.S. and Canada would tell me that they recognized their friends in the book—people I had never heard of. And I was able to keep track of which authors in the genre were being difficult by who Appin Dungannon was reputed to be. His identity kept changing in the popular mind-set.

Bimbos of the Death Sun was intended to be an observation of the culture of fandom, and a gentle warning. Science fiction writers build castles in the air; the fans move into them; and the publishers collect the rent. It's a nice place to visit, but please don't try to live there.

That said, welcome to Jay Omega's castle. Read on . . .

—Sharyn McCrumb
October 1996

CHAPTER 1

THE VISITING SCOTTISH folksinger peered out of the elevator into the hotel lobby. When he pushed the button marked "G," he naturally assumed that he would arrive at the ground floor of the building. Now he wasn't so sure. Things were different in America, but he hadn't realized they were *this* different. Perhaps "G" stood for Ganymede, or some other intergalactic place. Who were those people?

A pale blue blonde wearing a green satin tunic stepped on to the elevator, eyeing his jeans and sweatshirt with faint disapproval. "Going up?" she said in her flat American accent. She looked about twenty, he thought. The elevator was moving before he realized that he'd forgotten to get out.

"You here for the con?" she asked, noticing his guitar case.

"No. I'm a tourist." He liked that better than saying he was on tour; it prevented leading questions that ended in disappointment when the American discovered: 1) that they had never heard of him, and 2) that he didn't know Rod Stewart. "What are you here for?"

She grinned. "Oh, you mean you don't know? It's Rubicon—a science fiction convention. We're practically taking over the hotel. There'll be hundreds of us."

"Oh, right. Like Trekkies." He nodded. "We have some of your lot back home."

"Where's home?" she asked, fiddling with the key ring on her yellow sash.

"Scotland." At least she hadn't tried to guess. He was getting tired of being mistaken for an Australian.

As the elevator doors rumbled open on the fifth floor, the departing blue person glanced again at his jeans. "Scotland, huh?" she mused. "Aren't you supposed to be wearing some kind of funny outfit?"

"Is Diefenbaker here yet?" asked Bernard Buchanan breathlessly. He always said things a little breathlessly, on account of the bulk he was carrying around, and he was always clutching a sheaf of computer printouts, which he would try to read to the unwary.

Miles Perry, whose years of con experience had made him chief among the wary, began to edge away from the neo-fan. "I haven't seen him," he hedged.

"I had a letter from him on Yellow Pigs Day, and he said he'd be here," Bernard persisted. "He's supposed to be running one of the wargames, and I wanted him to look at my new parody."

Miles swallowed his exasperation. It was, after all, the first hour of the convention. If he started shouting now, his blood pressure would exceed his I.Q. in no time, and there were still two more days of wide-eyed novices to endure. Diefenbaker *would* encourage these eager puppies; he brought it on himself. Miles had a good mind to post a notice in the hotel lobby informing everyone of Diefenbaker's room number. Maybe a few dozen hours of collective neo-fans, all reading him fanzine press at once, would cure him of these paternal instincts. Really, Diefenbaker would write to *anybody*. Just let someone in Nowhere-in-Particular, New Jersey, write in a comment to Diefenbaker's fan magazine, and Dief would fire back a friendly five-page letter, making the poor crottled greep feel liked. More comments would follow, requiring more five-page letters. Miles didn't like to think what Dief's postage budget would run. And this is what it came to: post-adolescent monomaniacs waiting to waylay him at cons to discuss Lithuanian politics, or silicon-based life forms, or whatever their passion was. If he weren't careful, he'd get so tied up with these upstarts that he wouldn't have time to socialize with the authors and the fen-elite. Miles would have to protect Dief from such pitfalls, for his own good.

"I don't think he's due in until tomorrow," he informed the anxious young man. "Of course, you might look around the exhibition rooms and see if you can spot him."

"But I don't know what he looks like!" wailed Buchanan, but Miles Perry was already disappearing into the crowd.

"Miles, I must speak to you!" In a green turtleneck sweater and medallion, Richard Faber looked like a champagne bottle; he could be equally explosive as well.

"Why, hello, Richard. How nice to see you." Richard and Miles were fellow players in an other-world Diplomacy game called Far Brandonia, in which players became heads of state of mythical countries, and engaged in war or diplomacy, all meticulously recorded in a mimeographed fan magazine called *Brandywind*.

At the moment, Miles and Richard were in détente, which called for scrupulous politeness and as little communication as possible. "Have you signed any treaties with C.D. Novibazaar?" Richard demanded.

"Why do you ask?" countered Miles pleasantly.

"Because he has an army sitting on my southern border, that's why! I thought he was going to lend it to me, but now I'm not so sure. Is Clanton here? What about Diefenbaker?"

Miles noticed a crowd around the registration table. Wendy would be needing some help. "Perhaps we can get together later when the chaos subsides, Faber."

"Novibazaar still has the Seal of Corstorphine, hasn't he? Have we decided yet whether that gives him control of the railroads through Gondal?"

Miles closed his eyes for dramatic effect. That was just the trouble with Faber, in the game and out of it. No patience and no tact. "Richard, I will get back to you when—oh, good lord, it's him!" He began to run toward the registration table, having just glimpsed a white cowboy hat bobbing about five feet above the floor.

Miles Perry parted the crowd with less than his usual smoothness, and bent to shake hands with the figure beneath the bobbing Stetson. "Mr. Dungannon, what an honor to have you here!"

"The pleasure is entirely yours!" snapped Appin Dungannon, sounding for all the world like a peevish

elf. His narrowed piggy eyes darted from one autograph seeker to another, and finally cantilevered
upward to glare at Perry's plaster smile. "Are you
going to get me out of here?"

"I'd be happy to escort you to your room, and we can
discuss the schedule." Miles turned to the pack of fans,
waving Appin Dungannon paperbacks. "You can catch
up with him later, people," he told them. "Let him get
settled in first." Picking up Dungannon's leather bag
and computer case, Miles steered the guest author
toward the elevator, talking soothingly of complimen-
tary liquor and bulk orders of his books. Perhaps by
the time they reached his room, Dungannon would
have calmed down sufficiently for Miles to ask him
about judging the writing contest.

Behind them, an unfortunately loud voice
exclaimed, "*He* writes Tratyn Runewind?" The elevator doors sealed out a chorus of "Shhhhs" from the
surrounding fen. That sentiment, seldom so untact-
fully voiced, was one of the great common experi-
ences in fandom: the shock of discovering that the
chronicles of the golden Viking warrior Tratyn
Runewind were written by a malevolent elf with a
drinking problem. Part of fen lore, to be imparted
to promising newcomers, was the lecture on How to
Deal with Appin Dungannon. He was susceptible to
flattery; willing to autograph books (even second-
hand copies—signature only); but he would not
discuss future Runewind books, and if questioned
about details on the old ones, he was likely to know
less about the book than the fan did. He had
probably not read it as often. The one cardinal rule
of Dungannontry was: never, never approach the

author while wearing a Tratyn Runewind costume. He had once hurled an entire stack of hardbacks and a water carafe at a Runewind imposter. Still, he was internationally famous, and his appearance at a con was a guarantee of good attendance, so con organizers suffered him gladly; besides, his atrocities made good anecdotes to recount at later cons.

"And we were hoping you'd judge the costume contest later this evening," Miles was saying to his scowling charge. "Just a brief little event."

Dungannon grunted. "Especially if you're male."

Wisely choosing to ignore this, Miles continued, "And for dinner tonight, I thought you might like to join me and Walter Diefenbaker. You remember Diefenbaker, perhaps, from Mysticon?"

Dungannon made a sound that might have been assent or the sound of a Kyle-dragon swallowing a village. "Anyway, we thought we'd take you to dinner, and then you can sign autographs or whatever until costume time. There'll be filksinging in Room 211."

"I am indebted to you for the warning," said the author with a little bow.

"Oh, one other thing. There is another guest author coming to the convention. Perhaps we ought to ask him along to dinner as well."

"Who?"

"He's a local guy, a professor at the university. Just had his first SF novel come out in paperback. Would you like to meet him?"

Dungannon produced a fanged smile. "Let him wait in line with the other groupies," he said, giggling.

Miles Perry sighed, sensing a nasty Dungannon legend in the making.

CHAPTER 2

DR. JAMES OWENS Mega looked again at the empty registration desk, and then at the inhabitants of the lobby, trying to decide whom to ask for help: the green pirate, the robot, or the giant insect. None of the above. Further inspection revealed an even more interesting individual: a portly, pleasant-looking fellow who reminded him of Winnie-the-Pooh. The interesting thing was that the fellow wasn't costumed as Winnie-the-Pooh; he was wearing rimless glasses and an ordinary tweed suit, but he looked like a Milne character anyway. He must have been born middle-aged, Mega thought. Probably in his mid-twenties now, but he'll still look that way at fifty. Not entirely a bad thing, though. Mega, an engineering professor, had the opposite problem: he was thirty, but librarians still mistook him for an undergraduate. At least I don't look out of place here, he thought. He looked again at the giant insect. But, then, who would?

"Winnie" had noticed his bewilderment and ambled over to chat. "Hello," he said, offering what Mega couldn't help thinking of as a pink paw. "Our registrar has gone to the ladies' room. Perhaps I can sign you up. Are you preregistered?"

"I'm not sure," stammered Mega. "That is, I'm expected."

The bear was all smiling patience. "You sent in your fee?"

"No, I'm James Mega." He waited for a beam of recognition, but none was forthcoming. Mega managed a modest smile. "I'm the guest author."

The smile turned to stricken consternation. "Dungannon cancelled?"

Mega winced. "Sorry. I should have said I'm *one* of the guest authors. I believe Appin Dungannon is still scheduled to appear." He had a sudden premonition of what the weekend was going to be like.

"I'm afraid I've been a bit of an oaf." The bear smiled. "My name is Diefenbaker, and I'm sure I'll like you better than *anybody* likes Dungannon. Let me just get you a name tag. James Mega, did you say?"

"Well, I have sort of a pen name," Mega murmured diffidently. "It's my initials, really. You see, I'm an engineering professor at Tech, and I got this idea for a problem involving the effects of sunspot activity on computers . . ." He felt as if he were taking his orals again, and that he'd never stop worrying the explanation. A few stray conventioners had assembled within earshot and were looking curiously at him, as if trying to decide if he were someone or not. Mega plunged on into the explanation. "I couldn't do the thing as a research project, because the conditions were purely abstract, so I decided to write it up as fiction, and a paperback house liked it. . . . I just sent it in for fun . . . and—"

"I know you!" cried a ferrety-looking youth in a green turtleneck. "You wrote *Bimbos of the Death Sun!*"

Dr. Omega hung his head. "Yes," he sighed.

There it was: his pride, his fictionalized exercise in pure reason concerning the effects of sunspot activity in relation to polymer acrylic on capacitive interaction among high-frequency microcomponents in thick film circuits. He had known that when Alien Books bought it, there would have to be some commercialization, but he hadn't bargained on being heralded as the author of something called *Bimbos of the Death Sun*. And the cover art! A female bodybuilder in a fur bikini sprawled in front of a computer terminal, clutching the leg of a white-coated man holding a clipboard.

Dr. Omega lived in fear that some undergraduate student in engineering would figure out who he was and bruit the news around campus. As it was, he checked all the book stores in town once a week to make sure that no copies had been slipped onto the local author rack. His pen name, which he'd been so pleased with at the time, now seemed entirely too obvious.

"So you're Jay Omega?" smiled Diefenbaker, shaking his hand again.

"Er—yes. Short for James Owens Mega."

"It has a good sound to it. Does it signify anything? I seem to remember something about *omega*."

"Oh, yes? Have you studied engineering?"

Diefenbaker waved his hand. "I pick things up here and there."

"It was a good guess. Jay Omega is an electrical engineering term for frequency times the square root of negative one. It's the *imaginary* part of an inductance, you see, and since I was doing a work of fiction . . ."

"Oh, very clever!" beamed Diefenbaker. "I should love to read it. Did we order copies for the con?"

Jay Omega reddened. "Well, actually . . . my publisher's publicity department doesn't pay much attention to me, and I couldn't persuade them to send any, but I got the local bookstore to order some copies for me from the warehouse." He glanced down at the large, bulging canvas suitcase propped up against the registration table.

"I see," said Diefenbaker faintly. He smiled again. "Well, I shall tell everyone to come and get an autographed copy from you. In fact, I'll buy the first one myself after we get you signed in."

"Thanks very much. Do you think you could tell me what I'm supposed to be doing?"

"This is your first con, isn't it?"

"Yes. It wasn't my idea, really, but a friend of mine . . . she teaches science fiction in the English Department . . ." And I'll get her for this if it's the last thing I ever do, he finished silently. He could picture Marion perched on the arm of his sofa, saying, "Your job is only half done when you finish the book. Nobody will read you if they've never heard of you. So, publicize!" She found out about Rubicon from one of the sophomores in her science fiction class, and before he knew it, "Jay Omega" was a featured guest—paying his own way, of course.

"Why don't I show you around a bit, and then we can see where they're going to put you for the autographing."

Jay Omega looked again at his tweed-clad companion. "Why aren't you in costume?"

Diefenbaker looked surprised. "But I'm a wargamer!" Seeing that this reply had not proved enlightening, he explained. "The world of fandom is divided into several subgroups, mainly into hard science fiction—people who would read your book, for example—and fantasy folk, who are into Tolkien, Dungeons & Dragons, and—"

"Appin Dungannon?"

"Exactly. They're the ones in cloaks and broadswords. The rest of us settle for small tokens of resistance." He pointed to a button on his lapel: REALITY IS A CRUTCH FOR THOSE WHO CAN'T HANDLE SCIENCE FICTION. "Do you play wargames, by any chance?"

"Ah . . . on the computer?"

"No. Board games. Strategy between players. *Diplomacy. Kingmaker. War in the Pacific.* No, I see you don't. How about SF? Who do you read?"

Omega thought hard. "I read something I rather liked once. About an alien spaceman who was stranded on the moon and was trying to get to what would have been prehistoric earth. Can't remember who wrote it. What was it called?"

After a few seconds of polite silence, Diefenbaker sighed. "*Inherit the Stars.* James P. Hogan. He's an engineer, too."

"Oh. I don't have much time for reading fiction, really. When I'm not doing my research, I'm usually in my garage taking a car apart." Usually Marion's car. He could never convince her that the Christian Science approach was not a viable one to auto mechanics: the car would not heal itself if left alone. You had to fix it.

Diefenbaker had an inspiration. "I bet you'll like the technical displays. We have a room of computer set-ups, air ionizers, and various other high-tech toys."

Omega grinned. "Lead the way."

"All right. Oh, by the way, Miles Perry, one of the con organizers, and I are supposed to have dinner with your fellow author. Would you like to join us?"

"With Appin Dungannon? Sure, I guess so." Even people who couldn't read had heard of Appin Dungannon. His characters had been borrowed for a Saturday morning cartoon series called *Dungannon's Dragons*, and cardboard displays in every drugstore and supermarket hawked the Runewind books. "I hope he won't expect me to have read his stuff, though."

Diefenbaker smiled. "Don't volunteer the information. He never talks about his work, anyhow."

The front doors of the hotel swung open, and a gaunt young man with matted black hair and burning eyes marched into the lobby. He was dressed in a floor-length navy-blue overcoat, with a guitar slung over one shoulder. Rasputin, thought Omega. A mixed crowd of turtlenecks and satin cloaks converged on the new arrival, chanting, "Monk Malone! Monk Malone!"

Omega admired the modest but genial attitude the young man took toward his admirers. He made a graceful celebrity, signing his name with a flourish on a couple of Rubicon programs. "What does he write?" he asked Diefenbaker. "Or is he an actor?"

Diefenbaker stopped in mid-wave. "Monk Malone? He's a BNF. I thought everybody had heard—oh, no, I guess you wouldn't. BNF stands for Big Name Fan. He goes to all the conventions, knows all the filksongs, contributes to a dozen fanzines. He's a household word."

Omega was still puzzled. "But what does he *do*?"

"You mean in mundane terms? When he isn't at cons? I think he's still a custodian at the hospital. He works every weekend that there isn't a con, so they're pretty good about letting him off to come to them."

Omega shook his head. A hospital custodian was posing for pictures with various costumed princesses. It still didn't make sense. "But what's he so famous for?"

"He's a fan," said Diefenbaker gently. "And he's very good at it."

The elevator doors opened just then, and Miles Perry shot out like the White Rabbit in Wonderland. He halted for breath in front of Diefenbaker and Omega, and pointed in the direction of the upper floors of the hotel. "Do you know what he wants?" he demanded.

"Dungannon?" asked Diefenbaker.

Perry nodded vigorously. "Who else?"

"Well . . . what does he want?"

"I don't know!" wailed Perry. "Something called Smarties and Yorkies. Drugs, I expect."

"No, Miles. It's British candy. Smarties are like M&Ms, and a Yorkie is a chocolate bar." Being a Canadian gave Diefenbaker an occasional cultural advantage over his more insular American colleagues.

Miles Perry slapped his forehead. "Great! Where am I supposed to get British candy on five minutes' notice?"

"Just tell Dungannon it can't be done," said Omega reasonably.

They both looked at him as if he were tap-dancing on a mine field. Miles turned back to Diefenbaker. "But, seriously, Dief, what am I going to do?"

Diefenbaker shrugged. "Mass appeal, I guess." Cupping his hands to his mouth, he bellowed out across the lobby, "We need some British candy, folks! Anybody got any? All help will be appreciated."

A wave of shrugs passed through the clumps of people, but after a few moments of silence, a blonde girl in a green tunic and blue body-paint approached them. "British," she said shyly to Diefenbaker. "Like . . . does that include Scotland?"

Diefenbaker hastily changed a snicker into an encouraging smile. "Yes, Kathy. Indeed it does. Why?"

She twisted her yellow sash and shifted from one foot to the other in an effort of concentration. "Well . . . like I met this guy today, you know, in the elevator, and he said he was from Scotland, but he wasn't dressed up or anything. He was just in regular old jeans. I'd say he was a mundane. But he might like candy!"

"I'll find him if I have to mind-meld the desk clerk!" cried Miles, hurrying away.

Diefenbaker thanked the blue lady with grave politeness and sent her on her way. "You see what I mean about Appin Dungannon?" he said to Jay Omega. "He probably doesn't even want the candy. I expect he's looking forward to the tantrum he's going to pitch when he doesn't get it."

Jay Omega smiled. "I was just thinking how nice it would be to be famous enough to be difficult."

The Scottish folksinger picked up another magazine. Suppose you didn't want to fix gourmet meals in minutes, lose ten pounds in two weeks, or redecorate your kitchen? What did you bloody read in the States? Magazines that were sold in brown paper wrappers, he supposed, but those were a bit of a bore as well. He thought of turning the television back on, but there'd be nothing at that hour except the soaps. When he had first arrived in the U.S. for his folksinging tour of the East Coast, he'd planned on being quite a dedicated tourist, dutifully spending his days on bus tours and consulting guide books. After a while, though, all the cities became as indistinguishable as the hotel rooms, and he stopped going out at all. He had thought of doing some sightseeing in Washington, D.C., since he was so close. But he was thirty miles away from D.C., with no car, dependent on a ride to the gig, stuck in another of those bloody hotels; the view out of his window looked like every other place he'd been: gas stations, fast food joints, and an endless stream of four-lane traffic. He still sent postcards off to Margaret in

Glasgow, of places he hadn't bothered to go and see, but he spent his afternoons reading magazines or watching telly, until it was time to get ready for his evening performance. Bloody boring it was, too. Didn't the Yanks ever get tired of "Auld Lang Syne"?

He decided to have a quick look over the arrangement of his opening song, but a knock on the door saved him the trouble.

"Yes?" he called out. "Who is it?" You never knew about crime in the States, even in good hotels—which this one wasn't, not with Martians in the lobby.

"Mr. McRory!" More tapping.

"I'm Donnie McRory!" he yelled back. "I asked who *you* were!" He decided to open the door. It wasn't likely to be autograph hunters in this god-forsaken—"Well?" he demanded of the burly young man on the threshold.

Miles Perry nearly lost his nerve, but the thought of Appin Dungannon's tiny face, purple with rage, spurred him on. "I'm sorry to bother you, sir, but I'm one of the organizers of the science fiction convention, and we had a sort of emergency come up. I . . . I was wondering if by any chance you had some British candy with you?"

Donnie McRory narrowed his eyes. "Would it be a scavenger hunt?"

"Oh, no! Our guest author at the convention has asked . . . demanded, really . . . that we get him some Yorkies and Smarties, and we were wondering if . . . if . . ." Miles realized how inane all of it must sound to someone not faced with Appin Dungannon's malevolent presence. "He's a very *famous* person."

Donnie McRory sighed. A very famous person. *He* played to sell-out crowds at the Glasgow City Hall, packed them in at every Edinburgh Festival for the last five years, had a couple of specials on the BBC . . . but this writer bloke was a "very famous person," and *he* was somebody to borrow candy from. The United States could be very bad for one's ego. He looked again at Miles Perry's anxious face. "Well," he said, shaking his head, "I can let you have a couple of Yorkies. Didn't bring anything else with me. Why don't you get him some M&Ms? They're pretty similar."

Miles accepted the chocolate bars as if he had just pulled them from a stone in suburban Camelot. "Oh, thank you! You've saved my life! Listen, if you'd like to come to the con . . ."

Donnie McRory waved him away. "Thanks all the same, but I'll give it a miss." Ah, well, he thought, closing the door, it will make a fine story to tell back home. "What did you do in America, Donnie?"—"I loaned chocolate bars to the Martians."—Ah, well. He picked up a magazine: LEARN TO SAY NO WITHOUT GUILT. Perhaps he ought to have a look at that.

CHAPTER 3

JAY OMEGA TRIED to stand still as Diefenbaker patted an adhesive name tag onto the pocket of his blazer. Out of the corner of his eye, he could see a mousy young girl in a harem costume talking earnestly to an Imperial Storm Trooper.

"Interesting outfits," he remarked to Diefenbaker.

"Much of a muchness," said Dief, shrugging. "All the girls who weigh less than one-twenty wear as little as possible, and the rest of them put on cloaks and medieval dresses to conceal their bulk. You get used to it. I'd invite you to judge the costume contest, but we're using that honor as a sop to Dungannon."

"I don't know anything about costume design, anyway," murmured Omega.

"Neither does Dungannon. He lets his gonads do the judging, which means that the Galadriel with the best cleavage will win. Oh, dear, I think you're about to be put on the spot as guest author."

Jay reached into his pocket for his felt-tip autographing pen, but before he could fish it out, he realized that the pudgy young man who had just walked up was holding a sheaf of computer printouts, not a

18

copy of *Bimbos of the Death Sun*. He managed a weak smile, hoping that this was not a Tech sophomore who had tracked him to the con with a Drop-Add form.

"Really glad to meet you, Jay Omega," wheezed the fan. "I've read your book."

Walter Diefenbaker glanced at the name tag, winced, and began to edge away.

"I'm a fellow writer, and I thought we could talk a little shop."

"What have you written?" asked Jay Omega. As soon as he said it, he realized that he might be talking to Stephen King, in which case he had just committed the worst blunder in con history, but instinct told him that this could not be so. Stephen King's presence would be heralded nonstop if he should so much as stroll through the lobby, and besides, Jay Omega was sure that if he ever did meet Stephen King, he would not be greeted as a fellow writer and invited to talk shop.

Bernard Buchanan began to rifle through his papers. "I publish a fanzine called *Apa-Lling*, and beginning in this ish, I have a parody of Tratyn Runewind, called "Scratchy Woodwind," and instead of a magic sword, he has an enchanted oboe. Get it? Woodwind?" He thrust a Coke-stained page into Jay Omega's hand. "Now in this one, he offers to give the Demon Emperor a blow job. Get it? Like the Pied Piper!"

Jay Omega flipped through the pages of *Apa-Lling*, because it seemed preferable to actually talking to the crazed being in front of him.

The fanzine, a grainy photocopy of a computer-generated document, featured on its title page a still from *The Day the Earth Stood Still*. In front of the Washington Monument, Michael Rennie as Klaatu stood with his robot, Gort, but the photo had been altered so that Gort had the face of Ronald Reagan. The caption, serving as the fanzine title, was: "Now That's APA-LLING!"

Omega turned to a page at random. The words PERSON TO PERSON were hand-lettered at the top in magic marker, and the rest of the page consisted of two columns of short messages, addressed to a name or a set of initials. Still trying to make sense of the page, he read a few:

"John and Pat: Hope you're no longer croggled by all the mundanes in 'Frisco. Remember, the Force is with you."

"Chip Livingstone: Thanks for your letter; great as always, but writing letters is such a hassle. Why can't you call? If bread is a problem, call me at work, and I'll call you back on the WATS-line. It would be easier to settle things without having to rely on the Post Offal."

"M.P.: Don't forget that in the British election of 1859, Italy was one of the few issues that solidly united the British Left. The Workers liked Garibaldi as a popular leader with an army; the Liberals liked bigger trading partners and the principles of nationality; and the Whig Lords approved of the climate. I know Browning wrote: 'Oh, to be in England now that April's here!' but he was in Italy at the time—and a good thing, too, since most Aprils in Britain are solid fog and rain. No wonder they conquered India!"

* * *

"Never mind that," said Bernard, peering over Jay's shoulder. "Read my parody. Chip Livingstone says it's brilliant."

Jay Omega blinked. "Who's Chip Livingstone?"

Bernard Buchanan looked shocked. *"You've never heard of Chip Livingstone?* Why he's a super-fan! He's a major contributor to a dozen fanzines, and he's ranked third in the wargamers' poll, and I've heard that he is a *personal friend* of Robert Silverberg!"

"Jay Omega is an author," said Diefenbaker gently. "You can't expect him to know fan politics."

"What is this stuff?" asked Jay Omega, still staring at the page of non sequiturs.

"APA's are soap boxes for people who can't get anyone to publish them," murmured Diefenbaker. "These are messages to individual subscribers."

Jay Omega blinked. "Then why don't they just write personal letters to each other?"

"Would you like to keep that copy?" Bernard persisted. "I was saving it for Walter Diefenbaker, but I can't find him anywhere."

"Perhaps he'll turn up later," Dief assured him, grasping Jay Omega firmly by the elbow. "We have to dash."

When they had put several clumps of warriors and slave girls between them and Bernard Buchanan, Jay Omega looked again at the grubby print-out. "I still don't understand what this is."

"Think of it as a chain letter for disturbed children," said Diefenbaker soothingly. "I doubt if you'll find Bernard's parody very entertaining, so you can either lose that copy or be prepared to dodge him for the rest of the weekend. Unless, of course, you fancy telling him the truth about his work."

Jay Omega slid the papers into an R2-D2 trashcan.

"Wise move." Diefenbaker nodded approvingly. "Let's hide out in the art gallery until he latches on to someone else."

"Did he want advice about his writing?" asked Jay, still trying to make sense of it.

"Not advice, really. Praise. And then he'd have wanted the name of your agent, and your editor's phone number, and a letter of recommendation to both."

Diefenbaker led the way out of the hotel's lobby, a marble-floored rotunda dotted with red plush couches and potted palms, and into a corridor which connected a cluster of meeting rooms used for conventions within the hotel. Small white cards attached to the hotel's printed map, labeled the Pocahontas Room HUCKSTERS, the adjoining Powhatan Room ART GALLERY, and the Thomas Jefferson Room at the end of the hall was marked HIGH TECH, indicating the computer display area. Past the vending machines and the rest rooms, a smaller meeting room, the Patrick Henry Nook, had been labeled PRIVATE, and was reserved for the use of Miles Perry and his fellow convention officials.

"These rooms are for the permanent exhibits," Dief explained. "The seminars and gaming sessions are scattered throughout the hotel in smaller meeting rooms, and tomorrow night's banquet will be upstairs in the auditorium. You'll find a map on the back of your program in case you need it."

He led the way into the art room, where six free-standing partitions had been set up, each holding a collection of paintings and sketches, which were framed or mounted, and bore the artist's name on an index card below.

Jay stared up at a picture of *Star Trek*'s Mr. Spock changing into a werewolf on a chessboard in space. Not Salvador Dalí, he decided.

"I like this one," Diefenbaker remarked, pointing to an oil painting of a unicorn beside a waterfall. "My taste in art is rather Victorian, I fear."

Jay Omega was staring at an orange spaceship arching above a red and silver planet. "I don't think the perspective is quite right on that one."

"Probably not. It's one of Eric Bradley's, and he's only fourteen. But very promising, don't you think? Part of the proceeds from Rubicon go toward an art scholarship."

"Umm." Jay Omega thought they might do well to invest in some psychiatric counseling as well, but he reminded himself that if he had any fans, these were they, and that charity was in order.

"Sometimes we have a professional artist come to the con as a special guest. Of course, we can't afford Boris Vallejo, but we did try to get Peter Seredy. He did your cover, you know. His style is unmistakable."

Omega nodded. Certainly is, he thought, but my book advance won't cover the price of a hit man.

After a long and thoughtful inspection of the metal-band sculptures, the Yoda soap carvings, and the pen-and-ink sketches of dragons, Jay Omega followed his guide into the more commercial sphere of

. . . he had heard the term *fandom*, but could one say *con-dom*? He snickered. One had better not.

"Hucksters' room," announced Diefenbaker with a wave at the chaos before them. "This is where you feed your habit—or wear it," he added, as a monk-robed individual brushed past them.

The guest author solemnly contemplated the colorful chaos of weapons displays, movie posters, comic books, and a thousand lurid paperbacks scattered across a dozen metal tables, each surrounded by an assortment of elves and aliens.

"I thought you said there were electronics exhibits," he said at last.

"Different room. We'll get there. I thought you might like to see if any of the dealers have your book. It would be kind of you to autograph their copies."

"I never know what to write," sighed Jay Omega.

"Oh, just a signature would do," Dief assured him. "But it would be very kind of you to put their names and the date in as well. Of course, I've never written a book, but if I did, I think I might write 'Thank you for reading me.' If anyone ever asked me to autograph it, that is."

Jay Omega thought it over. " 'Thank you for reading me.' Yes . . . that would be good." He remembered Marion's stern lectures about publicity. He certainly hadn't received any promotion help from Alien Books. Even the mall in his parents' town hadn't been told about him. Marion said that Alien Books ought to be in charge of national defense, because they were so good at keeping secrets.

He edged his way past a Dorsai and said to the first book dealer, "Do you have any books by Omega?"

"Matheson," said the dealer promptly, pulling out a hardback.

"I beg your pardon?"

"Richard Matheson wrote it. *The Omega Man*. A movie starring Charlton Heston. They changed the ending, though. The original title was *I Am Legend*. This is a first edition."

"No, that's not it."

"Hmmn. Kane Omega, *Cosmic Sex*, Lyle Stuart, 1973."

"No. That's not it, either."

"I see you have my Runewind series," said a solemn voice behind him. "Shall I autograph these for you?"

Jay Omega turned around with outstretched hand. "Appin Dun . . ." His voice trailed away.

The young man behind him, a few inches taller than Omega himself, wore a white satin tunic and a wool homespun cloak. His bone-white hair fell to his shoulders, and his green eyes burned with intensity. He stood spread-eagled in white tights and scuffed leather buskins, one hand resting on his broadsword, and smiled benignly at the mortals in his path. With graceful dignity he accepted Omega's outstretched hand, which was still dangling in the air as he gaped.

"No," he smiled gently. "I am not He Who Writes the Saga, but He Who Lives It. I am Tratyn Runewind, Lord of the Eildon Hills, Wielder of the Red Gold Sword of Cu Chulainn, son of Aiofe and the Runewolf—"

"Dog meat if Dungannon sees you," Diefenbaker remarked. "You know how he feels about people impersonating his character, Cliff."

The Presence lifted his chin and endeavored to look noble. "The Scribe's envy is an affair for his soul, not mine," he intoned.

"He threw a water carafe at you at World Con," the bookseller pointed out.

"He once chased a Runewind down three flights of steps with a battle-axe!" said the Dorsai.

"Of course, he did!" snapped the Rune Warrior. "That was an imposter!"

"If he hears that you've been offering to autograph his books, you'll probably die from the aftershock of his rage."

"Well, I may change after the costume competition," the warrior conceded.

Diefenbaker was about to continue the discussion, but at that moment Miles Perry appeared, waving two packs of Reese's Pieces and three Yorkie bars. "I got them!" he announced breathlessly. "The Scotch guy said this would work."

Diefenbaker frowned. "I think some of the colors are different."

"Which ones?"

"I'd have to think about it."

"Come on, then. You get to sort them out. He wants them in twenty minutes."

Diefenbaker cast a helpless look at Jay Omega, as he was being dragged away. "I'll be back! Perhaps someone else could show you the gadget room . . ."

Left unattended, Jay Omega decided to spare himself the further humiliation of inquiring after his book. Instead he would find the gadget room on his own. A poster-sized map taped to a pillar in the hucksters' room provided reasonably clear directions. A large red arrow in the lower right-hand corner was labeled YOU ARE HERE. In the lower left-hand corner, a facetious physicist had penciled in, YOU MAY BE HERE. WERNER HEISENBERG. Omega smiled. After so much uninterrupted bewilderment, it felt good to get the joke. He took this as a hopeful sign that things would make more sense among the computers.

"Dr. Mega!"

Among the computer displays, air ionizers, and laser models sat Joel Schumann, a junior from last semester's microprocessing class. Omega groaned inwardly. He should have known that this would happen. One of his students had turned up at the con, and would soon discover the professor's guilty secret: *Bimbos of the Death Sun*. He might be able to swear Joel to secrecy, though. Omega took the offensive. "Er, what are you doing here, Joel?" the professor asked innocently.

The lanky blond grinned and tapped a computer monitor. "I came to look after these babies. They're on loan from the campus computer center. I volunteered because I thought it might be fun to come to this thing. See a couple of old sci-fi movies, watch the goings-on, and swap information with other hackers. What about you, Dr. Mega?"

Jay Omega managed a weak smile. "It's a long story, Joel."

CHAPTER 4

APPIN DUNGANNON STARED at the vacant gray screen of his computer terminal, as if he were waiting for the darkness to roll up on one side and reveal glowing letters of wisdom on the other. He tapped out $C = 1/\sqrt{\mu_0 \epsilon_0}$ while waiting for other inspiration to occur, but the exercise did not make him feel any closer to creation.

Beginning a stint of typing was always the most difficult part of writing a book. Once he got going, his brain projected a mental movie of the action onto the computer screen, so that he was not so much inventing as recording what he visualized. He could do maybe fifty pages a day on automatic pilot once he got going, but it was the getting going that was the hardest part. The early chapters of the book were like trying to carve the Gettysburg Address on Mount Rushmore with a toothpick; by the denouement, which was his current fixation, he had pretty much lost interest in what the story was about anyway, so it was even harder, if that is possible, to get it up for the task. He sighed inwardly, wishing, as always, that he hadn't already spent his publisher's advance.

Maybe it would help if he threw something.

Appin Dungannon had written twenty-six books about Tratyn Runewind. Or maybe he had written one book about Tratyn Runewind twenty-six times. He could no longer remember why the series had seemed like a good idea to him, or how he had felt about the first half dozen. It was as if he'd awakened one day to find himself manacled like Marley's Ghost with garishly covered paperbacks, a line of Runewind action figures (for which he received a percentage that was obscenely low), and a loathsome cartoon series, of which his cut was so meager that he'd fired his agent for the insult.

He was rich enough, according to his accountant— certainly his tax bill seemed to bear that out; and he supposed he was famous enough. He got fan letters in Elvish, and execrable unsolicited manuscripts to "please recommend to your publisher." He used those under his cat's dish, and by the phone for scratch paper.

Appin Dungannon was not as happy as perhaps a legend ought to be. His books were best sellers in the genre, but beyond that they went unread. He could expect, at best, a paragraph in *Publishers Weekly*, and he was always bypassed for the major SF awards. Dungannon fiddled a bit with the brightness knob on the monitor. He would have traded ten thousand costumed autograph hounds for one gilt-edged monograph on "Dungannon's Use of Celtic Mythology in Contemporary Fantasy."

At the moment, though, he didn't feel much like a synthesizer of Celtic mythology: he felt like Milton's God in *Paradise Lost*, and his Satan had him by the throat. Tratyn Runewind, Tratyn Goddamn Rune-wind, with the flowing white locks and the clean-chiseled features of a sea hawk. Dungannon scowled. It must have been some kind of sick fantasy, he decided. The five-foot-one schmuck with the Mickey Rooney face writing Viking bullshit. He was sure that the vermin discussed its psychological implications endlessly behind his back. There wasn't much he could do about that, except to cordially despise them, but, by God, he could make them keep out of his sight with their infernal Runewind get-ups. The very sight of some faggoty adolescent in tights and tunic made his hands itch for something to throw.

Dungannon glanced at his watch.

Someone was taking him to dinner soon, he thought. He supposed they'd expect him to talk to them. He reached for the bottle of Chivas Regal, and poured himself half a glassful. That ought to fuel a couple of paragraphs. It just wasn't *fun* anymore. The first books had been carried by his curiosity about the folklore, and when that ran out, he'd enjoyed putting his editors and his ex-wife in the manuscripts as monsters, but even that became dull after a while. Now he wrote out of inertia, and because they kept waving money at him. And the letters kept coming: scrawls of praise for the series, and pathetic little drawings of "Tratyn Runewind," but he went on writing, anyway. Because he couldn't turn down all that money; because he was afraid that stopping would dry up the gift of words; and because the serious novel in the typing-paper box wouldn't sell to anybody. He couldn't give it away. But for Runewind they would pay the earth.

Appin Dungannon took a stiff swallow of Scotch and stabbed a wavering finger at the keyboard. With a giggle of defiance he pressed ESCAPE.

No one had come back to claim Jay Omega for any con-related duties, but he was quite happy to be left to his own devices. In this case, the devices were various pieces of computer software which he and Joel Schumann were trying out one by one.

"These disks with burned protection sectors are a pain to copy," Joel remarked, tapping a few keys.

Jay Omega looked over at the screen to see if anything had happened, but a large, familiar brown suitcase was suddenly positioned between him and the monitor. Near the handles, where the zipper wouldn't close, copies of *Bimbos of the Death Sun* leered at him from their canvas confinement.

"I thought I'd find you here. *These* were chucked under the registration desk, quite abandoned. So was the smaller suitcase containing your clothes. I had that sent up to your room."

"Hello, Marion," said Jay, hoping he didn't look as foolish as he felt.

"I might have known you couldn't be trusted in the same building with gadgetry," she sighed. "But have you done *anything* to promote your book?"

"I asked the booksellers if they had it."

"And did they?"

"Er—no."

"And did you offer to provide them with some autographed copies? . . . I didn't think so. Well, perhaps we ought to find somebody who knows what guest authors are supposed to do." She grinned up at him. "How do you like my costume?"

Jay Omega eyed her warily. This type of question wasn't his forte. Let him compliment her new hairstyle, and it would turn out that she'd changed shades of lipstick. At present, Marion was wearing her dark hair in some sort of smooth flip style—he was sure that was different—and she was clad in a black jumpsuit. He was about to risk further humiliation by asking if it *were* a costume when the penny finally dropped. *"The Avengers!"* he cried. "You're Mrs. Peel."

Marion was pleased. "Not much resemblance to Diana Rigg," she said, shrugging. "But she was always my idol. I guess while other girls my age wanted to be Mary Tyler Moore, keeping house in New Rochelle for Dick Van Dyke, I wanted to be Emma Peel, going off with some terribly clever man who treated me as an equal, and having adventures."

Jay Omega pointed to the milling crowd of spacemen and Middle Earthlings. "Will this do?"

She handed him the battered suitcase. "Thank you, Mr. Steed. It will."

Marion led and Jay followed, which was pretty much the way it had been since that day eighteen months ago, when a shy young man in jeans and sneakers had appeared in the English Department with a spiral-bound computer printout, asking to speak to someone about science fiction.

Dr. Marion Farley, who had been in the office checking her mailbox, had given him a disinterested once-over, and said, "Sorry. The class is full. Tell your advisor to put you down for spring quarter."

The young man had quietly explained that he really didn't need the course, since he was already an assistant professor in electrical engineering, but that he would like to talk to someone about his book.

Before Marion had finished apologizing, he had invited her out to lunch, and over a couple of roast beef sandwiches at Bogen's, he explained to her that he had written a novel, based on a theoretical problem in engineering.

"You see," he'd said, finishing off the last of her potato chips, "the story involves a sun that emits rays causing slow but steady brain damage. But it affects only the women at the research station."

Marion, one of the more outspoken members of the Women's Network, gave him a wary nod. "Go on."

"The really important thing is that it affects the computers. What I'm actually concerned with is the effects of sunspot activity in relation to polymer acrylic on capacitive interaction among high-frequency microcomponents in . . ."

"The really important thing?" said Marion. "The really important thing is the *machines*, not the women?"

Sensing that he had said something wrong, he halted his narrative. "Well . . . from an engineering standpoint, I mean. What do you think?"

What did she think?

Marion thought that James Owens Mega was an ugly duckling who had not noticed his transition to swandom. She was sure that he had been a runty undergrad who had spent all his free time rewiring circuits, and who made good grades because he'd had no social life to distract him. She recognized the type from her own student days, when she'd hung around the wargames club, where it was okay for a woman to be smart and not pretty. Thank God she'd outgrown her pariah phase, she thought, adjusting one amethyst earring. Substituting aerobics classes for lit classes had done her a world of good. She'd gotten out of a miserable marriage to a fellow outcast who was going to remain in grad school forever, and, freed of the guilt of surpassing him, she'd earned her Ph.D. in two years. Now, in a new job at the English department at Tech, Marion had finally reached the stage of accepting herself as both smart *and* pretty.

She looked at her lunch partner, who was unselfconsciously finishing off a butterscotch ice cream cone. He must have filled out a bit since his scraggly adolescence, and the contact lenses he'd gotten "for better peripheral vision" did wonders for his dark eyes. He'd probably worn safety glasses before, she thought, and he'd have looked like a mosquito in them. Marion looked at his hair, the color of the butterscotch, and at the fine bone structure of his face. He's adorable, she thought. And he hasn't been notified.

"Are you still thinking about the plot?" he asked again.

"What? Oh, the plot. Why don't you leave the novel with me, and I'll read it and let you know. Actually, the idea of women getting progressively stupid is pretty exciting from a publisher's standpoint. It feeds the male hostility toward the competitive modern woman." She looked at him closely. "Did you do that on purpose?"

He blushed. "No. I just threw that in because I realized that some diseases are sex-linked, and it seemed plausible. My main concern was the computers."

Marion sighed. "It would be."

By the time Marion had tinkered with the characterization in his novel, and advised him through rewrites, chapter outlines, and query letters, he had become used to her, in much the same way that a stray cat gets used to belonging to someone. Marion had used a similar method of "taming": no sudden moves, a calm and friendly manner, and regular offers of food. She hadn't completely conquered his shyness, though. Marion sometimes felt just before they kissed that he was gearing up for it as one might approach the high-dive—with careful planning and much trepidation. She thought he was making progress, though. And his diffidence was certainly preferable to the first-date lunges of other professors she'd been out with, the post-divorce swingers.

Marion told herself that she was too happy in her newly won independence to be comfortable playing second fiddle to a male engineer earning three times her salary. Anyway, what if one of them got tenure and the other didn't? Marion had seen too many academic couples break up over tenure problems. If the university denied tenure to a professor, he or she had one year's grace period, and then it was: find another job. If your specialty was Chinese art or mining engineering that next job might not be anywhere close by. Usually in a relationship, if she got tenure and he didn't, you could kiss the marriage goodbye; the male partner's ego usually saw to that. Anyway, when faced with a choice between a lifetime of job security or a marriage with no guarantees, most people chose the job. She didn't want that kind of pressure built into her relationship with Jay. And maybe in two years, she would know what she wanted.

So marriage wasn't discussed. They didn't talk about the future, but neither of them dated anyone else, either. She didn't want to do or say anything that might change what they had. Marion knew that she often acted brisk and bossy, and that her tendency toward sarcasm made her seem tough and self-sufficient. She was afraid, though, despite her best efforts, that Jay Omega knew how much she loved him.

In the hospitality suite, Diefenbaker was just finishing the last of the yellow Reese's Pieces. They had been removed from the candy dish, because Smarties did not come in that color. Dief thought it was an exercise in futility anyhow; surely Dungannon would notice that there weren't any pink or purple candies in the dish, a dead giveaway that they weren't Smarties, and even if he failed to notice, one bite ought to give the game away. No one could mistake a peanut butter filling for a chocolate one. In any case, said Miles Perry, the Great One barely glanced at the ersatz British candy once it was rushed into his presence. No doubt he had a dim recollection of demanding it.

The hospitality suite television was showing a videocassette of *Forbidden Planet*, but no one was there watching. Most of the convention guests would not arrive until early Friday evening, and those who had come already were busy checking in, looking up old friends, or visiting the exhibits and game rooms. Toward the wee hours of the morning, when there were no competing sessions, a few of the faithful would gather to watch *Star Trek* episodes, and the couches would be taken by crashers who hadn't booked a hotel room. Diefenbaker occasionally allowed floor space in his room to an impoverished friend, but this time he'd decided to hold out for peace and quiet. He was going to be besieged by people as it was, what with so many Far Brandonians in attendance.

Since Diefenbaker lived in Ontario, most of his fellow gamers had to rely on correspondence and a severely limited phone budget for contact with him. Rubicon, his yearly foray into the U.S., was their only opportunity for a face-to-face meeting, and, to the limits of his civility and endurance, they were determined to make the most of it.

"Aha, I found you!" said Richard Faber, blocking the doorway. "That only leaves Chip Livingstone."

"You make it sound like a scavenger hunt." Diefenbaker smiled.

Faber began spreading photocopied maps over Diefenbaker's table. "There's an army on my southern border," he announced.

"I know. I put it there."

"I know, but—"

"You asked me to."

Faber turned crimson. "That was before I found out that C.D. Novibazaar was acting as minister of state for Emily of Gondal. That changes everything!"

A teenage boy with the word NOMAD scrawled on his forehead walked into the room just then. "Who's C.D. Novibazaar?"

The only thing Richard Faber liked better than to argue was to lecture. With a missionary gleam in his eye, he rounded on the newcomer. "Cambrecis Desmoulins (de) Novibazaar was a Hungarian refugee who held various posts in nineteenth-century French government. Just before the Peace of Campo-Formio, when Napoleon's arrival in Vienna seemed imminent . . ."

Having now received enough information to know that Novibazaar could not be read, smoked, or played on a PC, "Nomad" tuned out the rest of the explanation and returned to his original errand. "Miles Perry said you'd know what to do with these," he said, handing a stack of papers to Diefenbaker.

Dief looked at the top sheet. " 'The Verdant Moon of Milos.' Entries in the Rubicon Writing Contest?"

"Right. Cover sheets with the authors' identities are stacked on the bottom. You gotta get 'em judged so we can announce it after the costume contest tonight."

"I thought Appin Dungannon was judging these. Didn't Miles ask him?"

"No. He was planning to bring up the subject when he showed Dungannon to his room, but after the Smarties and Yorkies tantrum, he lost his nerve."

"Oh, more's the pity," said a disappointed Dief. "I

don't suppose it would have done any good to ask. Judging a writing contest is such hard work and, um, Dungannon does rather prefer the sexual possibilities of a costume contest. All right, I think I know someone who will judge the manuscripts. Where is Miles, anyway?"

"Orbiting the hotel, more or less, trying to be everywhere at once. He said something about meeting you for dinner. Didn't say where."

Diefenbaker looked at his watch. Just over five hours to get the manuscripts read and judged, Dungannon to entertain for dinner, and a hundred other minutiae to accomplish in between. He wondered if he ought to take a pill now, or wait for the headache to arrive.

"Richard, I really must go," he said, scooping up the manuscripts. "Why don't you talk to Bonnenberger?" He nodded toward an inert form on a straight chair near the window.

Joseph Bonnenberger, shirt buttoned up to his chin, four pens in his pocket, and 10W40 hair, sat squinting at a Rubicon brochure, apparently in preference to actually attending any of its events. Eventually his obsession with the Diplomacy game would force him from his lair into actual interaction with others of his species, but a breakthrough of this magnitude was still hours away.

Faber gave Dief a look of horror. "Talk to Bonnenberger?" he hissed. "The guy's a remora!"

Most people knew better than to talk to Joseph Bonnenberger, because he was indeed like the remora, a fish whose dorsal fin is a suction disk allowing it to attach itself more or less permanently to larger creatures. No one was willing to risk being civil to Bonnenberger, because it might result in their having to struggle through the rest of the weekend, dragging the bloated personality of the human remora in their wake. With Bonnenberger, it was best to limit oneself to pleasantries; anything more than that could be fatal.

"I'd rather drink Falstaff!"

Diefenbaker smiled pontifically. "Yes, Faber, but you deserve each other."

Before Faber could think up a reply, he was gone.

Not much had changed in the lobby. Diefenbaker noticed that "Filksinging with Monk Malone" had been chalked in on the announcement board for eleven P.M. He decided to let Miles handle the hotel management on that score. His own primary concern was to unload the contest manuscripts before he had to read them himself. He was about to set off for the computer room when he spotted a dark-haired woman seated off in a corner behind a small mound of *Bimbos of the Death Sun*.

When he approached the table she seemed so pitifully glad to see him that he bought a copy just to spare her feelings. "I was really looking for Dr. Omega," he said.

"He went in search of a Coke machine," Marion told him. "If you want him to autograph your book, leave it here, and you can drop by for it later."

Diefenbaker hesitated. Surely he couldn't just dump the manuscripts without getting Omega to agree to do them, but a glance around the lobby had shown three people waving frantically for his attention. As quickly as he could, he explained the problem to Marion, who smiled encouragingly, and assured him that Jay Omega would love to judge the writing contest. More reassured than perhaps he should have been, Diefenbaker scurried away.

Miles Perry had been cornered in the hall by a *Star Trek* officer and a heavy-set young woman with a serenely pretty face.

"We need to talk to you about the wedding," said the blue-shirted young man.

Miles blinked, trying to summon up a Rubicon program from his memory circuits. "Er—ah?"

The couple glanced at each other uneasily. "It's all set, isn't it?"

"What?"

"We are going to get married tomorrow night after the banquet in a *Star Trek* ceremony."

Miles Perry looked at the young man's dark hair, cut square across his forehead. "Spock and . . . ?"

"Saavik," said the bride. "We'll put our ears on later. Anyway, we wrote to ask about doing this, and we got a letter from Chip Livingstone saying it would be okay." Her voice quavered. "It is, isn't it?"

Miles Perry frowned. No one had bothered to notify him about any of this. He wondered if Diefenbaker were playing godfather to this. This Chip Livingstone business was getting out of hand! Still, it would provide a bit of drama, and perhaps some local publicity for the convention—not a bad thing. He studied the careful copy of the *Enterprise* science officer's uniform, and wondered if the bride would be similarly attired—in which case she might be mistaken for the planet Venus.

"Uh . . . Do you have a minister?"

"Yes. One of the campus chaplains has agreed to come over and perform the ceremony dressed as Captain Kirk."

"Splendid!" Miles wondered if the local paper would send someone on short notice.

"And my bridesmaids will be dressed as Yeoman Rand and Nurse Chappell."

"Best man?" asked Miles Perry, fascinated in spite of himself.

"Ensign Chekov," said the groom. "We couldn't find an Oriental, but my roommate is a *Bullwinkle* freak, and he does a great Russian accent. Boris Badenov."

"Okay, let's see if I can find you a room for that hour," said Miles. "Is that all you need?"

They glanced at each other again. "Well," said the bride softly. "There is just one thing missing."

Miles Perry nodded. "I think I can help."

CHAPTER 5

As Jay Omega opened the door to his room, a bound manuscript hit the wall near his head, and slid to the floor in front of him. "I didn't realize hotel rooms made you so jumpy," he remarked to Marion, who was sitting in the middle of his bed surrounded by papers. Most of the floor was covered with typed pages as well, he noticed.

"Idiot!" muttered Marion, consulting a clipboard. She scribbled furiously for several seconds before looking up to see Jay Omega, still in the doorway, poised for flight. "Oh, hello," she said. "I'm becoming dangerously homicidal."

"Yes, but your aim is bad."

Marion grinned. "Come in. You're safe. At least, unless you wrote one of these."

"I hope not. What are they?"

"They're the entries in a short-story competition they want you to judge. I thought I'd have a look at them. After all, I *teach* science fiction." She glared at him defensively, as if she expected him to object.

He nodded at the papers strewn on the floor. "Interesting grading system. What do you think of them so far?"

43

"The ones that landed near the bathroom are Bad Tolkien imitations or transcripts of a D&D adventure; bad Herbert, Heinlein, and Asimov are below the television; and these on the bed are the ones whose authors I want to hunt down personally and slap." She extracted a laser-printed manuscript in Gothic lettering from a pile on the pillow. "Listen to this . . .

> *Starwind, with her flaming hair about her shoulders and a red harem costume of sheerest Polarian silk, looked as seductive as any of the Rigelian slave beauties Hawker had seen in* Astro-Porn Magazine.
> *She tugged at her purple belt of passion. "My father, the president of the galaxy, said that I should make you welcome, Hawker-of-Earth."*

"Bad color sense," said Jay Omega, trying not to grin.

"Shut up! You know exactly what's wrong with this! It's a throwback to the Thirties teenage space-opera stuff. It's a stroke book!"

"Would you mind reading it again?"

Marion ignored him. "Or how about this one? It's called—are you ready for this?—'Goron: Alien Mercenary', and it's set three thousand years in the future. Listen:

> *Goron was grim as he faced the President of United Earth. 'This came in the mail yesterday,' he told her, setting the envelope and check on her desk.*

The blonde picked up the check and looked at the signature. 'Warlord Yoon! I thought he was dead!' She tore the check into tiny pieces. 'I wouldn't want the cleaning woman to find this.'"

Jay Omega blinked. "Three thousand years in the future?"

"That's what the author says," nodded Marion, tapping a line of typescript.

"And they still get mail? We don't even do that on campus. I leave messages for people on the computer mainframe, and they just check their file once a day. Electronic mail. Instantaneous."

"You don't send messages to me like that."

"No, just to other engineers, mostly. But eventually the English Department will catch on, and I don't think it will take three thousand years. Two thousand, tops." He ducked another manuscript.

"Did you hear what he called the 'President of United Earth'? *The blonde!* I'd like to use that kid's vertebrae for wind chimes!"

"His technology is absurd, Marion. Checks? Direct deposit banking is becoming a way of life now. Three thousand years in the future there's no telling what they'll be using, but it won't be paper checks."

"Did you notice the bit about the cleaning woman?"

"Good point. Machines should be doing all the maintenance work by then. I don't think he's thought out his civilization very carefully."

"I don't think he's ever met any women," grumbled Marion. "Too bad your book got titled *Bimbos of the Death Sun*. It's the perfect name for half these stories."

"I think it's too bad about the title, too," said Jay Omega softly. "Do you think my book is chauvinistic?"

Marion sighed. "Of course not. We've been through that before. The title isn't your fault."

"It's strange to be the author of something called *Bimbos of the Death Sun*, with pictures of female barbarians on the cover." He shuddered. "If the campus chapter of Women in Engineering ever finds out . . ."

Marion touched his arm. "It's a good book. For hard science fiction, that is. It's scientifically sound; it isn't pretentious; and I made damn sure it isn't demeaning to women. That's saying a lot for this genre. People who read it will know it isn't trash, no matter what stupid title they give it or what the cover art looks like. Science fiction is notorious for that kind of thing, anyway."

He nodded. "What are Appin Dungannon's books like? Have you read them?"

"They're thrust upon me. Sophomore computer science majors with bad skin and zero interpersonal skills are always wanting to do theme papers on Tratyn Runewind. They're not fiction, they're wet dreams. But don't tell him I said so at dinner tonight."

"Oh, Lord! Dinner! Should I change?"

Marion smiled. "Not unless you brought shining armor."

Appin Dungannon narrowed his piggy eyes as he contemplated the menu. The stuffed trout was expensive enough, but nauseatingly wholesome, and he was on the lecture circuit too much to ever order chicken voluntarily. What did that leave? Prime rib . . . the local specialty: peanut soup and Virginia ham . . . He didn't want them, either.

His nearest table partner, that Diefenbaker person, leaned over the menu and said, "Don't worry about time. The costume competition doesn't start until nine."

Appin Dungannon grunted. "The costume competition doesn't start until I'm *there*. However, I am ready to order. I think I'll have the trout. White goes with fish, you know. It'll go with my vodka." He held up his glass in a mock toast to them and giggled.

Diefenbaker and Miles Perry exchanged worried glances. The Eminent Pro had shown no signs of mellowing out as the evening wore on. His eyes glittered more as he talked, and he kept smiling in a none-too-reassuring way, but he still reminded them of a pinless hand grenade, and they couldn't be sure how many seconds were left.

Across the table Jay Omega and Marion were smiling nervously, and acting as if they were at the birthday party of a hyperactive child. Conversation was forced.

Dungannon had dismissed his fellow author by saying, "Haven't read your paperback. Doubt if I'd like it."

Once the orders had been given to the hovering waiter, he turned his attention to Marion. "Aren't you a little old for a femmefan?"

Marion's eyes narrowed. "I teach science fiction at the university."

Dungannon looked pleased. "Who's required reading?"

"Clarke, Brunner, Le Guin—"

"Heinlein?"

"The early works. And in the fantasy course, we teach C.S. Lewis, Tolkien—"

"Tolkien! Ah, so you do mythology? What about British myths?"

"Yes, of course. There's an excellent book based on Celtic lore. The students love it."

Appin Dungannon smirked. "Which Runewind is it? *The Singing Runes? The Flag of Dunvegan?*"

Marion raised her eyebrows. "No. As a matter of fact, it's *The Mists of Avalon*, by Marion Zimmer Bradley."

Dungannon took a hefty swallow of vodka, and everyone else at the table began talking hurriedly about the next *Star Trek* movie/Carl Sagan's novel/ and the rumor that the PC would soon be obsolete. Marion went back to her salad with the air of one who has performed an unpleasant task only to discover that she enjoyed it.

Jay Omega, who had never managed to feel like an author anyway, felt no sense of kinship with his fellow writer. He could think of nothing to talk about, and the idea of provoking Dungannon's ill-concealed wrath made him even less likely to talk than usual.

Miles Perry, who would have liked to have discussed convention business with Diefenbaker, felt compelled as host to keep up a flow of bright chatter. He had launched into a long and pointless account of Far Brandonian weaponry, to which no one listened, but the drone of his voice was soothing, and relieved everyone else of the obligation to talk.

Diefenbaker turned to Marion. "Is Dr. Omega one of those terribly sane and steady engineers, or does he have writer's quirks?"

Marion thought about it. "You mean like Balzac having to wear a monk's habit and write by candlelight? Jay isn't temperamental at all, but I don't know about engineers being sane and steady. The first time I went to his house, I found a radio in the refrigerator."

"There was a perfectly good reason for that," said Jay Omega. "Sometimes there's an intermittent problem in the radio, something that goes away when the unit heats up, and those problems are very difficult to detect. If you put the radio in the refrigerator, the problem will usually become permanent, and then you can fix it."

"Sounds reasonable," Diefenbaker conceded.

"Yes, but he also has lemons in there that are old enough to vote."

Jay Omega smiled. "I eat out a lot."

Appin Dungannon, apparently deciding that the attention had strayed from him long enough, announced to the table in general: "I think the roots of human behavior lie in the distant past, not on some silly planet out in deep space. In the heroic sagas like Beowulf, Elric of Melnibone, and of course, Tratyn Runewind, there are metaphoric implications . . ."

And all the women are cheeseburgers, thought Marion, spearing a piece of asparagus with her fork.

Dungannon's harangue continued for several

more minutes, while everyone concentrated on cleaning their plates, occasionally nodding fervently to maintain the illusion of interest. Finally Dungannon wound down, noticing that his dinner was almost untouched. Taking a last swig of his vodka martini, he leered across the table at his fellow author. "Well, that's enough about me!" he declared. "Now let's talk about you. Which one of my books did you like best?"

The Scottish folksinger propped one buskined foot on the bed and studied his reflection in the mirror. His dark suede trousers and laced linen shirt made quite a swashbuckling costume, quite in keeping with his repertoire of traditional Celtic tunes. People were always asking him why he didn't wear a kilt. "Because I'm not Harry Bloody Lauder!" was his invariable reply. Nobody seemed to realize that the whole kilt business was thought up in the early nineteenth century, and that it was the Englishmen who'd been given Scottish peerages who wore them. Perhaps he ought to say a word or two about it in his patter between songs.

He was scribbling a reminder on the song list taped to the guitar neck when he heard the tapping on the door. Donnie McRory glanced at his watch. An hour before show time. No reporters had asked for an interview. He hadn't ordered room service. Having run out of guesses, he flung open the door.

"Not the bloody Martians again!"

A blue-shirted Trekkie with pointed ears stood clutching the hand of a behemoth in a white tulle gown. Both were smiling up at him with an anxious cheerfulness. About twenty-three, he decided. Too old to be parading around in dress-up.

"Ooh, I love your costume!" said the girl. "Who are you supposed to be? Tratyn Runewind?"

Donnie McRory's jaw tightened. "I am not a part of your perishing convention! Now, was there something you wanted?"

They nodded solemnly. "It will take a little explaining," said the boy. "May we come in?"

Donnie McRory waved them toward the bed. He didn't suppose they had brought back his Yorkies. "Well?"

"We're getting married this weekend."

"Oh. That's magic, innit? Well, all the best. Here's luck, and all that. Decided which planet you'll live on yet?"

The bride frowned. "We were hoping you'd do us a big favor. It's very important to us."

Donnie McRory smiled expectantly, but he was thinking: Does he need help to carry you over the threshold, dear? I should think six blokes ought to do it, same as pallbearers.

The smile froze into place as they described their *Star Trek* wedding, with Chekov for best man and the minister dressed as Captain Kirk. "And the one thing we need to make the wedding absolutely perfect is—"

"Beam me up, Scotty!" cried McRory, suddenly remembering. "It's that phony Scot on the program you're wanting me to impersonate, isn't it? The one with the vaudeville Glasgow accent?"

"He's from Aberdeen," said the groom.

"Aberdeen Proving Ground, maybe. He's not a Scot!" McRory insisted.

"Yes, sir, but you are, and it would be so wonderful if you would just come and be him for the ceremony. It's a short little ceremony, really . . ." They looked up at him pleadingly, like demented puppies.

He scowled at them. "When is it?"

"Tomorrow night! You mean, you will?"

I'll dine out on this one, thought Donnie McRory. But it did beat reading the stupid American magazines or watching the telly. Tonight's concert was the usual one-nighter and he was booked into this bleeding hotel for the entire weekend. "I don't have to do anything else, but just be there?" he asked menacingly.

"Well . . . do you play the bagpipes?"

"Do you own a kilt?"

The social hour preceding the costume contest seemed to Jay Omega to be a cross between a worship service and a Senate investigation. As a relatively small fish in the literary pond, he had ample opportunity to observe Appin Dungannon in intellectual combat.

Dungannon, his ego weatherproofed with vodka, held court in front of a table of Dungannon paraphernalia: hardbacks, paperbacks, Runewind posters, action figures, and game spinoffs. The transactions involving these items were managed by a clerk, whose existence was beneath Dungannon's notice.

The encounters did not often go as Jay Omega had expected. As a new author, he had pictured public appearances in which faithful readers, their faces shining with admiration, would approach the author shyly and murmur what a wonderful book he'd written. The actual author/reader dialogues fell far short of his fantasies.

"You Dungannon?" asked a tall red-haired youth in armor.

"Correct," said Appin Dungannon, without bothering to look up from his autographing.

"Well, I just finished your last book and I don't think you ought to have killed Beithir in the last battle. I mean, sure, he threw the Sword of Ossian into Black Annis' Well, but he did save Tratyn Runewind from the Gabriel Hounds, and—"

Appin Dungannon skewered the fan with an arctic stare. "What's the matter with you, pinhead? Don't you have a life? If you enjoy meddling, join the Peace Corps!"

Another fan turned up with a stack of Dungannon novels. "Would you sign all these, please? Just a signature is okay."

"There are a few people behind you. Doesn't it bother you to be so selfish?"

The fan shrugged. "Not particularly. I figure this is my big chance to get your autograph."

"You have three copies of the same book in here."

"Right. Someday you'll be dead, and I'll be rich."

The crowd moved back a little in order to dodge flying hardbacks, but the outburst was not forthcoming. With a grim smile, Dungannon signed each book in the stack. When he had finished, the speculator snatched his copies and hurried away.

Two signatures later, just as a scrawny youth in G.I. camouflage was criticizing Dungannon's last book, a howl went up from the other side of the lobby.

"You little creep!" roared the guy with the stack of books. "You ruined my books!"

Dungannon leered at him. "You said signature only!" he yelled back.

"Look at this!" wailed the fan, holding out a book for the bystanders to see. "He signed 'J.R.R. Tolkien' on every goddamned one of them!"

"Who's next?" purred Dungannon.

No one wanted to discuss plot mechanics with Jay Omega. No one seemed to have heard of the book. Several fen ambled up to the table and examined the cover, which always made the author profoundly uneasy. "Er—it isn't really like that," he murmured to a young woman in a harem costume with a worried frown.

She tossed him a coy look. "Dirty old man!"

Even worse were the people who approved of the book, based only on its cover. One pizza-faced youth gazed longingly at the amazon in the cover art, and whispered hoarsely, "I think I'm going to like this one. Is it really raunchy?"

Marion snickered.

"No," said Jay Omega earnestly. "It's really very scientific."

"No explicit sex?"

"Not even close," Marion assured him. "Jay's idea of a stag movie is *Bambi*."

The young man wandered away, and several more fen, like browsing cattle, edged up to the book table.

"Do you make a lot of money writing paperbacks?" asked a Dorsai.

"No," said Jay Omega. "Hour for hour, the Seven-Eleven pays better."

"Do you have an agent?"

"Uh. Yeah." Her husband was from the same hometown as his college roommate; but only Marion had been trusted with that secret of how he got his big break in publishing.

"And what's your agent's name and phone number?"

Jay Omega was still wondering how Appin Dungannon would have fielded this question when Marion leaned over and said, "Never ask an author that, unless you want to be taken for a complete jerk!"

"Well, I have this great manuscript . . ."

Marion turned to Jay Omega. "What's your consulting fee in engineering?"

"For companies? Two hundred and fifty dollars a day, but—"

"Fine." She smiled up at the would-be author. "He'll read your stuff for two hundred and fifty dollars. In advance. Next!"

Joel Schumann, on a break from the computer displays, pulled out his wallet. "Is this your book, Dr. Mega! Hey, great! Would you autograph it for me? Boy, I can't wait to tell the guys in the lab that—"

"No! You can't do that!" gasped Jay Omega. "Look, Joel, what if I give you a book, autographed and everything. Will you not tell anybody I wrote it?"

He blinked. "Well, sure, I guess, Dr. Mega. If that's what you want."

"It is, Joel. It really is. Here, take the book. Now, is that 'Schumann' with two 'N's?"

"Yes. Say, Dr. Mega, are you coming back to the computer room?"

"Tomorrow for sure," he promised, avoiding Marion's disapproving glare.

"You're hopeless," sighed Marion, when Joel was gone. "All you want to do is play with your high-tech toys. You ought to hire someone to be Jay Omega for you."

"Someone like that?" asked Jay Omega, nodding toward his fellow author.

Marion looked at Appin Dungannon, who was posing for a Polaroid photograph with two barbarian maidens in leather battle garb. "Forget I mentioned it, Jay."

CHAPTER 6

THE RUBICON COSTUME Contest, held in the hotel ballroom, was the social event of the evening. Since no audience participation was required, except lust, which was optional, even sociopaths like Bonnenberger chose to attend. Wargamers, Dungeon Masters, NASA freaks, comic book junkies, and other assorted fen, costumed and otherwise, sprawled in metal folding chairs facing the stage and waited for the pageantry to begin.

As official judge of the competition, Appin Dungannon was given a seat of honor in full view of the stage, and a small table with refreshments and a yellow legal pad, on which he might make notes about the various contestants. At the moment, however, he seemed more interested in the lint on his cowboy hat than he was in the proceedings at hand.

Miles Perry, who was master of ceremonies, clutched his notecards in a sweaty fist, and glanced toward the wings. "Are they ready yet?" he mouthed at Diefenbaker.

Dief shook his head vigorously, and made a little sign that meant "Stall them."

Miles tapped the microphone. "Ah . . . hum. Can

you hear me out there?" An electronic shriek accompanied his voice, sending two technicians scurrying for the sound system. "First of all, I'd like to thank . . . I'D LIKE TO THANK . . . Testing."

"The costumes are really works of art," whispered Marion to Jay Omega. "It's rather sad, really."

"Why? I think it would be nice to have such . . . talent," he said almost enviously.

"I was thinking of how they use it, Jay. Imagine working for six months on a costume that you'll only get to wear once or twice a year, instead of going into dress designing or some other profession related to that skill, where you could actually accomplish something."

Jay Omega smiled. "Not everyone has a tenure-track mind, Marion."

"I still think it's a waste." She looked up at the stage where the first contestant had made her entrance. "And that is particularly a waste."

The costume was impressive: yards and yards of green velvet, carefully embroidered with gold thread and artificial pearls. A leather cummerbund with crisscrossed laces cinched the waist, and the white satin bodice stopped quite abruptly to expose two aggressively prominent breasts. The effect of this medieval artistry would have been pure enchantment, had the ensemble been ten sizes smaller, and had it not been battened on to a fierce-looking redhead who might have outweighed the average calf.

"This . . . ah . . . this is Brenda Lindenfeld of Annandale, portraying the Welsh goddess Arianrhod." Miles Perry's voice made little puffing sounds in the microphone as he leaned over his notecards.

The audience waited in polite silence—or perhaps weary indifference. No catcalls rang out from the darkness, and even Appin Dungannon remained solemnly bent over his legal pad, although the time he had spent evaluating the costume could be measured in milliseconds.

"I'm glad nobody laughed," murmured Jay Omega.

"Oh, no, they wouldn't," Marion assured him. "These guys know what it's like to be outcasts; they are very tolerant indeed. Except intellectually. Besides, look around you."

Jay Omega glanced toward the rows behind them, wondering what he was supposed to notice. "Yes? Looks like one of my engineering classes to me."

"It would," grinned Marion. "Mostly males. Women are at a premium in this hobby, and therefore even the plain ones are prized. That poor creature up there could pick up six guys by Sunday if she chose. I expect she'll settle for one."

Jay Omega peered at Brenda Lindenfeld, who was rotating slowly to show off her hooded cloak. "Any six guys?"

"No, silly. Any six losers. You know, the terminally shy guys who have no idea how to talk to a woman; the runty little nerds that no one else wants; and the fat intellectuals who want to be loved for their minds. She can take her pick of those."

"That's nice. I guess."

Marion shook her head. "I find it very frustrating. It seems to me that they all cluster together like sheep with their backs to the wind, when they would be a good deal better off coming to terms with the world."

"They seem happy enough," said Jay Omega, wishing somebody would laugh or applaud to prove his point.

"Sure, they've moved their egos into fictional bodies on the paperback rack so that they can ignore the rejection in real life. I teach science fiction, Jay! I know these people."

The second contestant, an Imperial Stormtrooper in a homemade uniform of cardboard and white Styrofoam clumped onto the stage. He pointed his laser-gun at the audience, leered menacingly through the white face mask, and bowed to Appin Dungannon. The judge's salute turned into a stifled yawn, and the Stormtrooper marched back into the wings.

Miles Perry leaned into the microphone. "And that was contestant number two. Chip Livingstone, as Sanyo the Stormtrooper." He clapped a couple of times half-heartedly, but the audience response was weak.

Marion turned back to Jay Omega. "I knew a guy once—Brian Something-or-Other—who had read every single book we covered in the science fiction course. He had also read every other book by the same authors. And do you know what grade he got in the course? An F. He didn't come to class half the time. He even missed the mid-term. He was off role-playing and dragon-slaying."

Jay Omega frowned. "That doesn't make sense. It's an elective course, and he knew the material. Why would he blow an easy A?"

"Beats me. I never could figure it out. A's don't mean much to a dragon-slayer."

"And yet . . . dragon-slaying does have its charms,

even for that rare integrated personality in the universe," said Jay Omega.

Marion looked at him like, who was he kidding? He was kidding her.

"You're right," she sighed. "I guess it bothers me so much because as an adolescent, I used to be one of these misfits. And in some ways, I guess I still am."

Jay Omega patted her hand. "You mean well, Marion, but you have the soul of an Old Testament prophet."

Walter Diefenbaker hurried down the steps at the side of the stage and scooted across to the empty chair beside Jay Omega. "I think things will take care of themselves backstage," he whispered. "So I thought I'd sneak out and watch."

The next contestant might have stepped off a book cover. It took the audience a moment's thought to realize that the perfect elf boy on the stage must really be a thirteen-year-old girl. Her smooth, dark hair was shaped to her head like a cap, and her slender body and small, pointed features suggested equally pointed ears beneath the hair. Her costume, vaguely reminiscent of Robin Hood, consisted of a puffed-sleeve shirt, leather jerkin and breeches, and fringed knee-length boots. Tied to her forearm was a stuffed satin dragon, positioned for flight.

Cameras flashed.

"This is Anne Marie Gregory of Reston, as a Dragonrider," Miles Perry informed the crowd. This time the applause was generous.

"She's excellent!" said Marion. "For once, a face that fits the costume."

"Quite talented, too," nodded Diefenbaker. "She

makes those dragons herself. There are some on display in the art room."

Marion glanced in the direction of Appin Dungannon, who seemed no more interested than usual. "I suppose she'll win?" she asked Diefenbaker.

Dief reddened. "Well, she certainly has a good costume, and she shows a lot of talent, doesn't she? We must hope for the best. Of course, judging is purely subjective, and—" His voice trailed away to the sound of two hands clapping—Appin Dungannon's hands, in fact.

A simpering little blonde of normal weight had wandered up to center stage and was smiling uncertainly across the footlights. Her long golden hair was crowned with a garland of silk flowers, and the elegant white dress was a wedding gown rescued from the Goodwill. She was the personification of cotton candy.

Miles Perry looked anxiously at the applauding judge, and then at the vision in white. "Ah ... we have here Miss Brandy Anderson as the lovely Galadriel from *The Lord of the Rings*."

Marion scowled at Diefenbaker. "Do you mean that this is going to turn out to be a beauty contest? Does it matter whether you made your costume, or how original you are?"

"Well," said Diefenbaker. "Sometimes it does."

"The blonde didn't make that costume. She just brushed her blonde curls and threw on a wedding dress!" Marion had spent too many years as an ugly duckling herself to approve of beauty winning out over merit.

"You mustn't rely too much on the judge's

objectivity," stammered Dief. "Still, the Dragonrider was well done, and I find that I'm never much good at predicting what people will do."

The next two contestants, a Gandolf in a velour bathrobe and a high-school-varsity version of Conan the Barbarian, drew a ripple of polite applause from the audience, but their appearances hardly disturbed anyone's conversation. Probably the most original costume of the evening was a tentacled alien, glistening with plastic slime, and belching smoke from his navel. He received loud applause from the audience, and a standing ovation from his roommates, but Dungannon waved him off with a sour smile. A short person in a monk's robe and a rubber Yoda mask drew some cheers from favoritism, but he rated no more than a glance from the judge.

"That was Matt Simpson from Laurel, Maryland, as Yoda the Jedi Master in *Star Wars*," said Miles Perry, as if anyone needed to be informed. "Our next entrant is Clifford Morgan, costumed as . . . oh, dear!" With a stricken look, Miles Perry dropped his notecards and fled behind the curtain.

In the ensuing fascinated silence, the audience could hear a murmur of voices rising from backstage, building to an occasional crescendo of shouting. After several moments of muffled argument, the curtains parted, and a tall, slender youth with a homespun cloak and snow-white hair appeared at center stage.

The audience gasped and whispered, as the contestant drew his sword and raised it in a salute to Appin Dungannon. "Writer of the Saga!" he cried. "Tratyn Runewind salutes you!"

Appin Dungannon looked as if he had just sat on Excalibur. He glared at the posturing figure on stage with the look of a fire dragon about to belch forth a wave of fire and sulphur: eyes bulging, nostrils flared, and face an apoplectic shade of purple.

With the possible exception of the immortal Rune Warrior, nobody breathed. All eyes turned to Dungannon. After an interval of suspended animation that felt to Marion long enough to do one's taxes in, the tableau exploded.

Appin Dungannon snatched up the nearest empty folding chair and hurled it at the stage. "You impudent maggot!" he roared, hoisting another chair over his head. "Out of my sight! Out of this con!"

"Tratyn Runewind" continued to smile as he dodged folding chairs, comforted perhaps by the knowledge that he had now become a legend in the annals of Fandom. Years from now, oddly dressed misfits would hunch over their Cherry Cokes, and between rolls of the eight-sided dice, they would tell the novices how Clifford Morgan had suffered abuse and risked untold real-life hit points from projectile folding chairs, in defense of the integrity of his player-character, Tratyn Runewind.

Fortunately, Appin Dungannon eventually ran out of chairs, and in the lull from bombardment, Miles Perry crept back on to the stage and half-dragged Clifford Morgan behind the curtain.

"But I wanted to ask him about his new book!" Morgan protested as he vanished from sight.

Appin Dungannon took his place behind the table as if nothing had happened. "Proceed," he said, pointing his pencil at the stage.

The Klingon admiral who appeared from behind the curtain was showing considerably more emotion than his race is purported to have. He stood white-faced and rigid before the footlights, as if anticipating a firing squad. When Appin Dungannon flashed him a benign smile and waved him off, the Klingon bolted for the wings, a performance that was, as Mr. Spock would say, "Highly illogical."

The remaining contestants strutted and fretted their minute upon the stage, barely noticed by anyone, except when Miles Perry, whose notecards were out of order, referred to a Batman impersonator as "a character who manages to be strong and yet beautifully feminine at the same time." The next contestant, Wonder Woman, hurried onstage, but the giggles and references to Robin and the batpole continued for several minutes.

Finally Miles Perry announced that the contestants had all been seen, and that after a few moments of deliberation, the judge would make his rulings known. Appin Dungannon pulled his cowboy hat over his eyes, and propped his boots up on the table.

"Do you really think he'll pick the blonde?" hissed Marion.

"I don't think he'll pick Tratyn Runewind," said Jay Omega.

Diefenbaker smiled nervously. "It isn't important. All the winner gets is an autographed copy of a Dungannon first edition and a gift certificate from Pizza Hut."

"It's the principle of the thing," grumbled Marion.

Jay Omega consulted his program. "It says they're

showing movies in here after this. Want to stay for them?"

"That depends," said Marion. "What's playing?"

"I'm not familiar with them. There's one called *Robot Monster*."

"That's a man in a gorilla costume and a diving helmet pretending to be an alien. And he keeps contacting the mother ship on a Jacob's Ladder from a high school science lab," said Diefenbaker.

"Fifties. Low budget," added Marion.

"Okay. How about *The Thing*? It says James Arness is in it. I liked him in *Gunsmoke*."

"Well, you won't recognize him here. He plays a giant asparagus who crash lands in the arctic."

"Hmm. *Plan Nine From Outer Space* . . ."

"Oh, no!" cried Marion and Dief together.

"Cardboard tombstones!"

"Hubcap flying saucers!"

"Bela Lugosi died while they were making the picture, and they kept the footage he was in, but they finished the movie with a replacement who looked nothing like him."

Jay Omega looked hopeful. Visions of the computer room danced in his head. "Well," he said, "I guess we don't have to see that."

Marion grinned. "Of course we do! It's so bad you won't believe it."

All entrants of the costume competition except the offending Runewind had lined up across the stage awaiting the judge's decision. Batman and Wonder Woman held hands, while Conan and the Klingon scowled at the audience. Yoda chatted with the Dragonrider.

Appin Dungannon pushed back his Stetson and took his feet off the table, nodding to Miles Perry that he was ready. Perry rushed over to receive the results, but Dungannon waved him away, and ambled toward the stage himself. The audience cheered loudly.

After adjusting the microphone some four inches downward, Dungannon smirked at the audience and motioned for silence. "Can it, you sleaze-puppies!" he said cheerfully. "Nothing you think could possibly make any difference to me. In fact, it would be news to me that you *did* think. Are there any Libertarian assholes out there?"

A few wargamers raised their hands.

"That's right. Raise your grubby little hands. You should all be belled, like lepers. Where was I? Oh, yeah. To keep from having to say this two hundred more times during this con while you grovel for my autograph: yes, I am working on the new Tratyn Runewind. In fact, I expect to be finished with it tomorrow, and since I am over deadline as usual, my editor will be coming here to pick it up."

Several members of the audience began to look alert.

Appin Dungannon sneered. "Stop salivating, vermin! You have all the creativity of a Spellcheck disk! I have told my editor not only to avoid you at all costs, but also to disinfect his overcoat after he leaves, in case some of you brush past him in the halls."

"I don't believe this!" whispered Marion. "He's alienating his fans."

Diefenbaker shook his head. "He's always like this. People expect it."

"Can you tell us about the new novel?" yelled a guy in the fifth row.

"No, pinhead. Your attention span isn't that long. Besides, I want all of you to save the quarters you receive for casual sexual encounters in the men's room, and buy the book. And after you have finished reading it, with your lips moving no doubt, I want you to write me a nice long letter saying exactly what you think of the plot, the characters, and every little detail—and use it for toilet paper! Because I don't want to hear from you morons! None of you can spell *literature*, much less recognize it!"

"Who won the costume contest?" someone called out.

"See what I mean about your attention spans? Shut up, cretin, I'm vilifying you. When I have finished abusing you, I will announce which of these poor afflicted sociopaths gets a free pizza to encourage his delusions." Dungannon shaded his brow with his hand and leered across the footlights at his captive audience. "A pizza! You people need pizzas like TWA needs terrorists."

Murmurs rippled through the audience.

Dungannon looked pleased. "I've wounded you? That's a promising sign. You're too stupid to leave, but at least you know when you're being insulted." He beamed at them. "By the way, I see according to tomorrow's schedule that some of you will be staging your own pathetic D&D variant at an ungodly hour, running all over the hotel pretending to be elves and things." He shook his head. "Isn't ridicule enough for you? Must you have contempt as well?"

The costumed fantasy fen booed gently.

"Oh, spare me your whines! I wish I could arrange for cannibalistic orcs to lurk in the halls and eat the lot of you, but—contrary to your delusions—that is not possible. So let me just warn you that any asshole who dares to disturb me during your morning antics, while I'm writing, will have an IBM keyboard for a suppository!"

Dungannon answered the catcalls and cries of "The plane! The plane!" (an oblique comparison of his size to that of Herve Villechaize) with a tip of his cowboy hat. When the hissing died down, he consulted his legal pad. "Now about the costume contest. May I suggest that next year's prize be a lifetime of therapy and the sedative of your choice? I came up with several possible categories of merit. Most Likely to Be Mistaken for a Dirigible . . ." He nodded in the direction of the velvet-gowned Brenda Lindenfeld who reddened and scowled. "Most Sexually Ambiguous. Most Ludicrous. Most Pathetic. An outstanding bunch; the competition was fierce. —But not for first place. That choice was quite simple. The winner is Miss Brandy Anderson as Galadriel."

The blonde in the wedding gown clapped her hands and rushed forward to hug Appin Dungannon amid faint applause.

"I don't believe it!" hissed Marion. "That old satyr!"

"I'm afraid it was no surprise to the rest of us," Diefenbaker reminded her. "Remember, it's only a pizza."

Marion nodded. "Didn't you say that the Gregory girl had stuffed dragons in the art show?"

"Yes, you can bid on them during the auction Sunday."

"Fine. I'll bid what I think the piece is worth *plus* the price of a large pizza! Somebody has to see that justice is done."

Jay Omega grinned. "Thank you, Mrs. Peel!"

"We said that we were going to announce the winner of the writing contest tonight," Dief reminded them. "Are you ready?"

Jay looked at Marion. "I think so."

"Give us a few minutes to confer," Marion told Dief.

When he had gone to alert Miles of the delay, she and Jay put their heads together. "Okay, I eliminated all the garbage and the written accounts of D&D episodes. Do you remember the three stories you read?"

"I remember what they were about, I think. I didn't have much time," said Jay.

Marion handed him a piece of paper. "I wrote down the titles and authors to refresh your memory. 'The Prodigies' is about the group of kids with ESP."

"Oh, right. That was pretty well-written. It looked like a lot of work was put into it."

Marion sighed. "Fiction shouldn't look like a lot of work was put into it. It should flow. But the story was okay."

"Which one was 'Memory Awake?' The computer that had killed the ship's crew?"

"Yes. The title is a line from Emily Dickinson: 'Remorse is memory awake.' "

"That's okay, isn't it?"

"That's wonderful, Jay. It shows a glimmer of literacy. And the grammar is better than the rest of them."

"I thought the technical material in that one was

well done. Some of the details I'd quibble with, but it held my attention."

"That's because it was hard science fiction. Your genre. But you're right. It was a good story. The last one is 'Elfsong.' It's fairly standard fantasy, but the author handles description beautifully. The writing is very strong, but the story is so-so."

Onstage, Miles Perry had finished presenting Miss Anderson her pizza certificate, and after urging a final round of applause for all the contestants, he gripped the microphone and looked inquiringly at Diefenbaker. Dief pointed to Jay Omega and nodded.

"One last award to be given tonight, folks. Our other guest author has very graciously agreed to judge the short story contest, and I'd like to get him up here to announce the winner. He's here as Jay Omega, author of *Bimbos of the Death Sun*. Let's have a big hand for Dr. James Owens Mega of Tech's own engineering department!"

Jay Omega stopped in mid-stride, looking stricken. The audience was cheering louder than ever, and Marion was motioning for him to go ahead. Oh, well, he thought, maybe I could make a living repairing sports cars in a specialty garage. He wished Appin Dungannon would throw a folding chair at Miles Perry. How did he know, anyway? Of course, Marion must have explained it all to the con organizers when she arranged for him to come as a guest; apparently his preference for anonymity had not been made clear enough.

He joined Miles Perry onstage. "Thanks very much for the introduction," he said, trying to smile.

"As Miles told you, I judged the short story contest, and there was certainly a wide range of entries."

Marion nodded. Bad Herbert, bad Tolkien, bad Stephen King.

"Choosing a winner was really a tough decision." I wouldn't paper-train a dog on most of them, Marion had declared. "I know you're all very serious about your writing, and that you put a lot of work into writing and rewriting your fiction." He grinned. "I know I do.

"Anyway, before I announce the winner, I want to wish all of you luck with your writing endeavors and to tell you to keep trying."

Because they need all the writing practice they can get, Marion finished silently.

Jay Omega consulted his list. "This year's short story contest winner, for 'Memory Awake,' is Diana Gentry."

Gasps and buzzes of conversation swept the audience. Finally, a cherubic fourteen-year-old boy in tights and tunic approached the stage.

Jay Omega took all the time allowed by the youth's approach trying to think of a diplomatic way to ask. No inspiration was forthcoming, and when the kid joined him onstage, Jay Omega blurted out: "You're Diana Gentry?"

He blushed. "No. She's my mom, and she's not here tonight. She teaches English at the junior high. You said the contest was open to anybody."

Jay Omega handed the boy a gift certificate from Blue Ridge Books. "Accepting on behalf of his mother . . ."

Marion shrugged. "An English teacher. It figures."

CHAPTER 7

"DID YOU KNOW that there's going to be a wedding at this con?" Miles Perry asked Diefenbaker.

"Mark and Linda? Somebody mentioned it to me. Their player characters are getting married in a D&D episode run by Jerry Larson tonight. Why? Do you want to go?"

Miles shook his head. "Not them. Somebody's having a *Star Trek* wedding tomorrow night after the banquet."

"Oh. Well ... surely they cleared it with you, Miles. You're director of the con."

"No. They say Chip Livingstone gave them the go-ahead."

Diefenbaker looked over his shoulder with a frown. "That is very strange."

"You're telling me," said Miles. "I guess I should have asked to see the letter."

"Yes," agreed Dief. "I hope they don't expect him to show up at the nuptials."

"I trust not, though it seems everywhere I turn these days, I trip over the name of Chip Livingstone!"

Dief permitted himself a snicker. "He's becoming quite the BNF, isn't he?"

"He certainly is! I heard a couple of neofans boasting that they were going to have breakfast with him!"

The laughter was louder at that.

"I should like to be there for that," said Dief. "And how about the *Star Trek* wedding—did you manage to work out the details?"

Miles nodded. "Yes, I have no objections. In fact it ought to be good publicity for the con. Maybe we'll make the front page of the city section this year."

"I'm glad you're pleased. I just hope there aren't any more surprises in the works. Appin Dungannon is quite enough spontaneity for one con."

Jay Omega had spent another half hour at his autograph table, thus earning at his present royalty rate another thirty-six cents in book sales, while Marion toured the hucksters' room. Presently she returned, pinning a calligraphy button to the pocket of her jump suit. It said:

> IF THEY CAN SEND
> A MAN TO THE MOON,
> WHY CAN'T THEY
> SEND ALL OF THEM?

"Don't take it personally," she told Jay. "I just thought it was cute. It will sustain me through the cheeseburger fiction I have to read from the more chauvinistic male writers."

"I don't have the energy to be insulted," said Jay

Omega. "Bewilderment is taking all my concentration. I keep hearing snatches of conversation as people walk by, and trying to make sense of them. 'Life on a breathable gas ring . . .' "

Marion nodded. "They were discussing a book by Larry Niven."

"Oh. I thought they were talking about a contaminated stove. How about this one? A 'real Monty Haul campaign'?"

"Dungeons & Dragons. Monty Hall hosted a give-away show called *Let's Make a Deal*. Gamers use the term to mean an adventure in which players get lots of treasure and easy victories."

"Good evening," said a young man in a broad-brimmed floppy hat, edging past them.

Jay stared at the young man's costume—a long, many-pocketed overcoat, and at the twenty-foot scarf dangling at both ends. "Who was that?"

"Quite correct," grinned Marion. "It was, indeed. Now, would you like to look in on the filksinging? It's nearly eleven."

He yawned. "Gee, is it eleven, already? Shouldn't we plan to turn in, since we have a lot to do tomorrow?"

Marion's face fell. "Oh, are you really tired? I was sort of looking forward to the filksinging."

"But you keep saying how ridiculous all this is."

She sighed. "Old habits die hard, I guess. I can remember sitting around singing defamatory *Star Trek* parodies until the wee hours of the morning.— Years ago, that is," she added hastily.

"And you keep saying how glad you are that you outgrew it," Jay reminded her.

"It might be fun," said Marion wistfully. "We don't have to stay long."

Jay Omega reflected guiltily on the times he'd made Marion spend an hour in the auto parts store, and of keeping her waiting twenty minutes for lunch while he did "just one more thing" on the computer.

"Okay," he said, "I suppose we could just stop by."

Stashing his books in the canvas suitcase, he followed Marion into the elevator. Its other occupant, a stocky teenager, was wearing army fatigues and a button reading:

BAN THE BOMB!

SAVE THE WORLD

FOR CONVENTIONAL WARFARE

Jay Omega decided that this was one of the wargamers Diefenbaker had been talking about.

"Where is the singing? Back in the auditorium?"

"No. It isn't a concert—just a sing-along. They'll probably have it in Monk Malone's room."

Jay remembered the Rasputin character who was "very good" at being a fan. "Yes, I've seen him," he said. "A sing-along, huh? Will we know the songs, do you think?"

"In a way," smiled Marion. "I guarantee you'll know the tunes. And the words will be passed around on mimeographed sheets." Seeing Jay's disconcerted expression, she added, "We won't stay long."

They emerged on the fourth floor, and threaded their way past a corridor D&D game. A stern-looking DM, surrounded by piles of reference books, was flip-

ping through something called a *Monster Manual*.
Five players sat in a circle, whispering among themselves. Two of them were in medieval costume, and a
third wore a button that read:

I'M NOT STUPID
I'M NOT EXPENDABLE
AND I'M NOT GOING!

Jay Omega decided that the young man's player
character must be a low-ranking member of the
expedition.

"I still say we ought to try the holy water!" hissed
the player in the brown cloak.

"Can't my character see through that wall?"
another demanded.

Farther along the passage Marion pointed to a
door with a DO NOT DISTURB sign looped on the door-
knob, and a larger one in calligraphy taped to the
door: DO NOT DISTURB! TRESPASSERS WILL BE VIOLATED.
"Appin Dungannon's room."

"I don't see how he can write at a convention,"
said Jay Omega.

"They pay him well," said Marion. "You, on the
other hand, make more from teaching summer
school than you will ever make from *Bimbos of the
Death Sun*, so you lack motivation."

Jay Omega wisely decided against replying. The
discrepancy between the salaries of engineers and
those of English professors was a sore point, and one
that Marion could not discuss in modulated tones for
more than two minutes. He noticed a piece of paper
under Appin Dungannon's door, and thought that it

must be nice to have such ardent admirers that they slipped mash notes under your door.

"Fan mail," sniffed Marion. "Not that he deserves any. That was quite a performance tonight."

"I think it was all part of the show," said Jay Omega. "I got to thinking how outrageous someone would have to be to attract any attention in this crowd, and I think Dungannon has hit upon one of the few ways to stand out."

Marion scowled. "He's an odious man. And the worst part of it was that most of the time I agreed with him!"

Jay had stopped walking, and seemed to be listening to something in the distance. A moment later, Marion heard it, too: the sound of Sixties folk music came wafting down the hall to meet them. They walked toward the sound and found the door to room 467 ajar. A few feet of floor space remained in one corner of the room, but the area around the double bed was thick with costumed adolescents. Monk Malone, in a Nehru jacket and Levi's, sat curled up on the bed, clutching an old Gibson guitar. Around him, mimeographed pages rustled, and the impromptu choir sang to the tune of "The Sloop John B":

> So put up the *Enterprise's shields*
> *Recharge the phaser banks,*
> *Beam up the captain on board,*
> *And let us go home . . .*

Jay Omega seemed to remember a Kingston Trio version of that song, having to do with a sailboat in the Caribbean. This version seemed to be about *Star*

Trek. He eased down into the empty floor space next to Marion, wondering if the room had fallen into a twenty-year time warp.

It couldn't be the beer. Donnie McRory was certain of that. If you sent American beer out to be analyzed, the lab would probably phone up and say, "Your horse has diabetes." Anyway, he hadn't had more than a pint or so. He lay on the bed, still dressed, listening to his headache and wondering if reading would make him drowsy. It seemed a bit early to call it a night, but he hadn't felt like staying around in the bar after he'd finished his set. Too many mellow and friendly Americans wanted to talk to him, but that always seemed to involve a discussion of American versus British tax plans or an offer of things he didn't want, usually illegal things. He'd decided to give it a miss.

Very tiring, being a tourist. Very lonely. Phoning Margaret was out of the question, too, because it was five in the morning in Glasgow.

As he lay on the bed in the darkness, faint familiar strains materialized in his head.

> *"And it's no, nay, never!*
> *No, nay, never no more . . ."*

In spite of his headache Donnie McRory chimed in, *"Will I play the wild rover; no, never, no more."* He sat up, wide awake. Hallucinating in an American hotel, was he? Nobody else was in town, he was sure of it. By "nobody else," he meant the Clancy Brothers, the Chieftains, the Corries, or any of a lesser-known assortment of blokes in white fisher-man sweaters billed as Celtic folk groups. But who else would be singing "Wild Rover"? Somebody was singing it. He was awake enough now to be sure of that.

Donnie McRory grabbed his guitar and his room key and headed out to investigate.

In Monk Malone's room on the fourth floor, the filksingers swayed in time to the music, and someone was slapping a tambourine to punctuate the chorus of the song: *"And it's oh,* (crash) *no,* (crash) *never . . ."*

The Cossack on the bed nodded approvingly. "Well done, my children. Now, one more time for Gordy."

> *"I've been a wild Dorsai for many a year,*
> *And I spent all my money on Saurian*
> *beer . . ."*

"I don't get it," whispered Jay to Marion.

"No," she replied. "And unless you are willing to read about two hundred science fiction novels, you never will."

Jay Omega sighed. "Tell me again why we're here."

Marion patted his hand. "It's a new experience for you! Don't be such a stick in the mud. Anybody who can sit through the entire graduation ceremony year after year, in his cap and gown, ought to be able to endure an hour of this. Besides, Jay, who knows? Maybe someday they'll compose a filksong about one of your books."

"Yeah, and it'll probably be *Bimbos*. I can imagine

what they'd pick. *'Wait 'til the sun shines, Dummy.'*"

The last strains of "The Wild Dorsai" had just ended for the second time when Donnie McRory appeared in the doorway. "The Martians," he muttered. "I might have known."

Monk Malone looked up at the newcomer, still in the leather Celtic costume from his act. "Nice costume, man," said the Monk. "Are you a Scadian?"

"No. I'm a Scot."

"I knew a Scadian Scot once. I think he was The Black Douglas. Anyway, his specialty was medieval Scottish warfare."

Marion whispered to Jay, "Scadian. Member of the S.C.A.—Society for Creative Anachronism."

Donnie McRory began to back away. "Yes, well, I just recognized the song you were singing, and came down to see what you were on about." Even American beer might be preferable to spending an evening with someone who thought he was The Black Douglas.

"That's a nice guitar, too," said one of the rug rats. "Do you play?"

After a moment's frosty silence, Donnie McRory decided that he couldn't pass up the challenge. *That's your trouble, Donnie,* Margaret would say. *You're an incurable show-off.*

"Off the bed w'ya," he said, shooing Monk Malone into the corner by the television. After a few experimental strums on the guitar, and the adjusting of a string or two, Donnie played the intro to "The Wild Rover."

Obediently the filksingers ground out: *"I've been a wild Dorsai . . ."*

The strumming ceased. "What was that rubbish you came out with?" he demanded. "Have you been monkeying with the words?"

Sheepishly they nodded.

"Right. Well, here's another tune. This one's about your friend Doug," he said to Monk Malone. He sang the first verse of "The Lammas Tide" amid a respectful silence. "There," he said, glaring at them when he'd finished. "Does anybody have any Martian words to that?"

Fifty negative replies.

"Right, then. Let's start again, you lot. In the key of G.

Now it fell about the Lammas tide . . .
When the muirmen whin their hay . . . "

Diefenbaker had been run to earth in the wargamers' conference room by Richard Faber, Bernard Buchanan, and two people he didn't recognize, but who would turn out to be Far Brandonian correspondents, he was sure.

"I'm really glad I found you," said Bernard Buchanan, still clutching his sheaf of computer printouts. "My parody is really coming along. In fact, I was hoping you might show it to Appin Dungannon . . ."

"Novibazaar!" said Richard Faber in his most non-negotiable voice.

"I have a question about the term 'Brudhorc,'" said one of the strangers.

Diefenbaker tried to look patient. "I don't have

any of my Brandonian files with me at the moment . . ." he murmured.

"Are you free for breakfast?" asked Bernard Buchanan.

Dief was prevented from expressing the conviction that starvation would be preferable to dining with Bernard by the agitated appearance of Bill Fox in the doorway. "Dief, man, you gotta come now! Somebody's yelling their head off in one of the upstairs halls, and it's going to disturb half the hotel."

The hostage was so relieved to be rescued from Far Brandonian politics that he nearly forgot to ask what the difficulty was, but at the last moment it occurred to him that the information might prove useful, and he inquired.

The messenger shrugged. "Beats me. Somebody on fourth is yelling about somebody having been murdered. They sent me to get you."

CHAPTER 8

As DIEF HURRIED out of the elevator on the fourth floor, he saw that Miles Perry and most of the crowd from filksinging had already congregated in the hall. The central attraction was a shouting match between the cloaked D&D player and another member of the party. Off to one side a forlorn young woman in a white tunic and slacks was clutching a packet of tissues, and sobbing loudly.

"You killed him!" shouted the D&D player. "I can't believe that. And they let you!"

Walter Diefenbaker, wise in the ways of cons, did not spare a glance in search of a lifeless body. Edging his way through the spectators, he planted himself between the two combatants, and waited for silence. When the recriminations had trailed away into a sullen silence, he said, "Do you realize that you could get all of us tossed out of this hotel?"

Behind them, the sobbing continued unabated. Dief glanced over his shoulder. "Will somebody go and buy her a Coke?"

Marion slipped out of the crowd and put her arm around the girl's shoulders. "Come on," she said. "You'll feel better if you talk about it."

The girl allowed herself to be led toward the elevator. "I didn't know what they were going to do," she sniffled. "But Mark is never going to believe that."

"What did they do?" asked Marion.

"Well, Mark and I were going to get married tonight."

"Your player characters?"

"Yes, of course. We'd been planning it for ages, and of course everybody who was in the game with us knew about it, and so did Jerry. He's the Dungeon Master. So tonight when we started the ceremony, Daciano the Red Dwarf—that's Phil Castellow's player character—killed Wolfgang Bartok, who is Mark."

Marion nodded sympathetically. "And you didn't know."

"No! But everybody else did. Phil must have been on the phone for hours setting all this up, and the DM had to have helped him. Before the ceremony, Daciano crept into Wolfgang's room and killed him, and then, using the Shapechanging Talisman from an NPC cleric named Laurence Talbot, he assumed Wolfgang's appearance."

"Did you know about it before the ceremony?"

The 'widow' frowned. "I did, of course, because as a player I hear Larry describing everything to us, but the point is that my character, Arianna of the Golden Wood, couldn't know that a switch had been made, so she had to go through with it in good faith. You have to play your character according to how they'd really act . . ."

Marion nodded as she thought, "And this, above

all, to thine own self be true . . ." She didn't think a handy quote from Shakespeare would be very comforting, though, so she didn't mention it.

Diefenbaker was still talking soothingly to the recently deceased bridegroom, and the crowd, giving up hope of a fistfight, began to drift away.

"It was fair in the game," erstwhile dwarf Phil Castellow insisted. "He should accept it as the will of the gods."

"You are slime, Castellow!" hissed the late Wolfgang Bartok. He had come dressed for his "wedding" in a gold tunic and matching tights, and a short blue-velvet cloak, all of which clashed with his red tear-streaked face.

Jay Omega, deciding that Marion would come back to the filksinging to look for him, wandered back to Monk Malone's room, where a band of faithful Celtophiles, mostly Scadians in medieval dress, still clustered around Donnie McRory. He had worked his way through "Annie Laurie" and "The Lewis Bridal Song," and was just beginning "The Skye Boat Song," when Anne Marie, the elfish Dragonrider, piped up.

"Do you have any songs about fantasy? We're kind of into that."

The others nodded. "You know. Dragons, fairies, ghosts."

"Oh, aye?" said Donnie McRory. "Just average Yanks, I thought you were." Still, after years of performing, he saw an audience's preferences as law, so he gave it a moment's thought. As he looked up for inspiration, Jay Omega slipped in the door.

"What was that din down the hall?" McRory wanted to know.

Jay Omega reddened, hoping that he wasn't about to be mistaken for a Martian. "Two of the fantasy gamers were arguing because one killed the other in the game."

"Ah. Character assassination." McRory grinned at his own joke. "Now getting back to this song you wanted. We have one about a soldier in the army of Bonnie Prince Charlie's, and he's on the point of death. Dying in England, far from his home in Scotland. So he tells his mate to go off without him, but that he'll be the one home first, because he'll be taking the way of the dead, the fairy route, which can be traveled in the twinkling of an eye." He paused for effect, pleased at the rapt attention of his audience. "We call that fairy way the low road."

"The low road," murmured the circle of listeners, shivering under the spell.

"Right. And here is the song about it." He strummed the guitar. " *'You take the high road, and I'll take the low road . . .'* Well, before we go into that one, would somebody go and get me a beer?"

Elsewhere in the hotel, Richard Faber's hands felt like the bottom of a beer bottle—cold, wet, and glassy—but his throat was dry. He was attempting the frightening and unfamiliar: a conversation with a human female approximately his own age. Brenda Lindenfeld was not, however, Richard Faber's own weight: she could have made two of him, and would still have had enough flesh left over to construct a standard-sized tapir. At the moment, this entire mountain of femininity was gazing at Faber with respectful attention, suggesting that it had been her life's ambition to hear a detailed account of the Battle of Leningrad.

Still dressed in her velvet gown from the costume competition, Brenda was an impressive, if not attractive, figure. She spent most of her time in the wargames room, which was too monotonous for other women to bother with, and the lack of competition prevented unfavorable comparisons. Besides taking care to be the only woman in the room, she smiled a lot. She had decided that Richard Faber had potential; he was, in real estate terms, a real fixer-upper, a bargain for anyone willing to put a little effort into the project. His hair looked like the floor of a service station, and his clothes would have been rejected by a reputable charity, but these flaws were easily corrected, she thought, with praise and successful management. The fact that Richard Faber was an obnoxious bore was more worrisome, but even that could be an advantage. There was considerable security in the knowledge that no one else could possibly want him.

Brenda Lindenfeld felt that security should be valued, if not above rubies, then at least above pleasant companionship. She endured more trauma on a daily basis than the Hershey Chocolate Company could ever hope to assuage. Children stared at Brenda when she passed on the street; people made remarks about her in public, seeming not to care if she heard them. They seemed to think they were giving her constructive criticism, or perhaps alerting her to a hitherto overlooked fact—as if it had somehow escaped her notice that she weighed two hundred and sixty-seven pounds.

Brenda Lindenfeld knew, all right. Her mother managed to mention it at least once at every meal, and her grandmother sent diet articles from *Family Circle* in her letters. Jobs other than those paying minimum wage, out of public view, were not open to her. People in high school hadn't wanted to be seen in her company—nobody's ego is secure enough in high school to allow a friendship with the class leper; guilt by association is the law of the teenager. So she cordially hated everyone in her class, and she ate to make up to herself for all the injuries she endured; and instead of having a social life, she read.

Brenda had discovered that reading is as close as you can come to teleporting. By identifying with the plucky elfin princess in a fantasy novel, Brenda achieved her own version of astral projection: she left the tank of flesh behind her, and lived for the duration of the book in free form, in a world where problems could be solved by magic and by swordplay, rather than by painful and boring exercise courses and diets of boiled rice.

When she turned twenty-three, still living at home and taking the occasional course at the community college to postpone Life Itself, as she thought of it, Brenda made another momentous discovery: a social life was possible. There were others like her. A hotel in Richmond had advertised a science fiction convention, featuring as special guest her favorite fantasy author, so Brenda had invented a speeding ticket to get the registration fee from her parents, and off she went.

The weekend had been a revelation. No one laughed. People in the fantasy seminars seemed to judge her by what she said, rather than by her looks. Brenda was inspired. She had stayed up late in the conference room, listening to a discussion of group marriage as described in Heinlein's book, *The Moon is a Harsh Mistress*. When she read it later, she realized that the boy who defended it had completely misunderstood the concept, and she wondered how the author would have felt about his book being prized as a rationale for promiscuity. But that night Brenda agreed enthusiastically, even reverently, with the speaker's premise; she was thinking maybe he would like to get laid. She didn't expect to have too many other chances.

That first encounter had been rather clammy and uncomfortable, and no relationship had come of it, since they had forgotten to exchange their real names, but Brenda knew that she was on the right track as far as life was concerned. Now work and the community college were simply time-killers between cons, a sop to her parents' expectations. She kept changing majors so that no one could be sure when she was supposed to graduate. This term it was Day-Care Management. It ensured parental good will and free room and board, leaving Brenda considerable spare time to establish her real life, as the goddess Arianrhod in the world of Fandom.

Brenda's latest project, Richard Faber, would pose no particular acquisition problem; and she was well aware of his other liabilities. As he continued to drone on about some stupid battle or other, she had sized him up sexually, and pronounced him not so much gay or straight as "ambidextrous"—in the literal sense of the word. It was the only option that had thus far afforded itself in Faber's nonexistent social experience. Unless she miscalculated—and practice with other members of his species made that unlikely—Faber was an over-eager but terrified virgin, who should be good for about two minutes of frenzied but uninspired coupling, and for an infinite amount of gratitude and devotion thereafter. Brenda didn't particularly enjoy sex, since all her experience thus far had followed this pattern, but like any pusher, she realized the value of the drug to the addict, and she profited from the affection that followed the high. It was quite amazing to her that such an inconsequential, messy little act could result in so much dependence and emotion. Quite magical, really. The goddess Arianrhod gloried in her mystic powers.

Thank God he knew so much about tactical warfare and diplomacy, Richard Faber was thinking. His explanation of the Battle of Leningrad had really fascinated this intelligent creature. At last, someone who respected him for his knowledge, someone who shared his interests. He grew more confident as he went along. She hadn't questioned a single one of his theories! He had patted her hand once when she'd said, "How interesting," and she hadn't pulled it away. In the back of his mind Faber knew that he should be trying to track down Walter Diefenbaker to settle matters about Novibazaar, but he couldn't bring himself to leave. Really, when you got up very close and looked into her large brown eyes, she wasn't bad at all.

Finally, with more courage than it took to aim your Zero at an aircraft carrier, Richard Faber managed to say, "We could continue this discussion in my room if you like." His palms felt like the sides of an aquarium.

For form's sake, Brenda Lindenfeld hesitated. The less experience she permitted to show, the better the spell worked. "Well," she said. "I suppose we could. I wouldn't want us to disturb anyone out here, but I just have to hear the rest of this. It's so interesting!" She hoped he wouldn't expect her to know which war he was talking about.

Faber sighed with relief. He'd done it! The conquest had been made. Another couple of hours and she might let him kiss her.

Brenda was thinking that it was about time he'd got around to asking her, and wondering when she should go and get her belongings from behind the curtain in the video lounge. Hotel rooms were expensive, and of course she hadn't booked one. She thought she could put up with another half hour of this drivel, and then she had to get him laid so that she could get some sleep. Late nights made her puffy.

Appin Dungannon was back in front of his computer monitor scowling at the words TRATYN RUNEWIND. The evening had not been altogether unpleasant. He had tossed and gored several obnoxious fans, and he had quite enjoyed the exercise of heaving folding chairs at an incarnation of his cretinous Rune warrior. He had been in quite a ven-

omous mood that evening, probably because of the
chapter he'd been working on before dinner, but now
it was time to write the most hackneyed part of a
Runewind book, the ending. He should be able to
knock it off in an hour or two, and that would leave
the early morning for proofing and final corrections,
which need not be too extensive. Some post-teen
English major enslaved to the publisher to proof
copy could go through and make sure that Runewind's horse was not black on one page and brown
on another. Really, he didn't know why they bothered. The demented fans who read the series had
hours of fun devising plausible explanations for his
sloppiest screw-ups. They would churn out endless
articles in their unreadable mimeographed excres-
cences trying to explain why Runewind's sword
changed lengths or why his mother was known by
two different names. So far, the two likeliest explanations—apathy and Chivas Regal—had not been
suggested.

He felt almost virtuous to be slaving away at the
keyboard in the small hours of the morning, especially considering that he'd had other offers. Several
of the less grotesque femmefans had hinted at a willingness to add a night with an Eminent Pro to their
list of celebrity memorabilia. Dungannon usually
declined these offers for a variety of reasons: proofs
of age could be faked, and lawsuits were a nuisance;
some of the girls might carry the Andromeda Strain
as well as having read it; and, most daunting of all,
he could never go through with such an encounter
without imagining the evening written up in a
grubby fanzine. "Is Runewind's Sword a Dirk? A

Blow-by-Blow Account of Appin Dungannon's Bed-
side Manner." The very thought of such an article
could cripple his strongest lust. And since the fen
had no more privacy sense than a bee and no knowledge of copyright, such an article once written would
be reprinted by every 'zine in fandom. It would be
harder to kill than the ax man in *Friday the Thir-
teenth*. Sleep alone, thought Appin Dungannon,
safety first. He hated the fen too much to give them
such a weapon. Might as well give a chimp a hand
grenade.

> *Tratyn Runewind gazed down at the mighty
> Runesword in his scarred left hand. At his feet, the
> gold-tressed warrior princess cowered, awaiting
> the inevitable blow. She would not plead for her
> life. Hers was a proud race, one that died with lips
> bubbling laughter and froths of heartsblood. She
> was very young.*
>
> *With a sigh of regret for the death-tide that
> flowed between them, Tratyn Runewind sheathed
> the red-tipped blade. "Live to fight again, my fair
> one," he said, pulling her to her feet.*
>
> *The girl-general narrowed round blue eyes
> in suspicious disbelief. What could the Celtic dog
> mean to do with her? Did he not know that
> she would grasp her own death gladly before she
> would submit to such as him?*
>
> *Runewind gave her a gentle push in the
> direction of the dragon-prowed longships. "Per-
> haps we will meet again in the woof of time. Go
> now."*
>
> *Fingering the hilt of his Runesword, Tratyn*

Runewind watched his enemy scramble down the path like a frightened and bewildered child.

When she reached the bend in the rock cliff, she turned and looked at him, hesitantly lifting her small white hand.

"Another time," whispered the warrior.

There were corrections to make, and other details to be attended to, but they could wait until he was sober. Appin Dungannon retrieved his disk, yawned, and watched the monitor screen go dark.

And so to bed.

Marion yawned. "Well, what did you think of your evening in Middle Earth?"

Jay Omega finished arranging the contents of his pockets on the dresser top. "Well, I wouldn't want to live there." He grinned.

"No. I don't suppose you would. But then you happen to be particularly well suited for this planet, lucky for you." She sat down beside him on the bed and began to rub his back.

"You seem to get along pretty well yourself," he pointed out, arching a shoulder blade.

"Just like my cat," she laughed, scratching the shoulder. "Are you going to purr?—I suppose I do get along well these days, but it was an acquired skill. In high school I was too smart and too puppy-fat to be anything but miserable. That was what made the SF group so appealing: we were all outcasts together. Even after all these years it stays with me. I can't help feeling that I get along in the world only because I learned what was expected and how to

go about things. Like Marco Polo in China—
functioning, but not really belonging. You, on the
other hand, seem to have been born knowing how
to cope."

Jay Omega nodded. "Like an IBM computer with
BASIC built into its ROM. No programming for it
necessary."

"Whatever that means." Marion frowned. "I suppose so. You enjoy all the things that other people
consider necessary evils—yard work, meetings,
teaching undergrads. I used to think you were a
saint, but after knowing you a year, I've decided that
saints aren't saints, either. They are just people who
happen to enjoy doing things the world approves of.
And sometimes I think to myself that if we'd gone to
high school together you wouldn't have asked me
out, and it annoys me—still!"

"I'd have been afraid to. You can be rather fiercely
feminist sometimes."

"At the moment, I don't feel that way at all. Are
you sleepy?"

"Not any more," said Jay. "In fact, I think I'll go
down to the video room. I heard they were going to
show *War Games* at midnight. It has a lot of computer technology in it. Want to come?"

Marion shook her head. I'll just stay here and take
a cold shower, she thought grimly.

CHAPTER 9

MILES PERRY COULD open one eye just wide enough to see a six and a four on his digital alarm clock. That meant he had been allowed at most three hours of sleep. He groped for the shrieking telephone, and managed to find it without making further demands on his eyes.

"Huh—what?" he croaked into the earpiece.

The responding voice advanced him three levels toward wakefulness.

"Yes, Mr. Dungannon! Good morning!—You want what?—Oh. Room service. I'm sure the hotel has it. Would you like me to give you that number? I could look it up."

He sat up now, wondering where the phone book would be hidden. "What's that, sir?—Well, no, I don't suppose the hotel room service would go to Burger King to get you an egg and cheese croissant. —Oh. I see. Yes, sir. It'll take me half an hour to get dressed. —Fifteen minutes, yessir. Fifteen minutes to get dressed. —And I should tap on your door to let you know it's there. —Certainly, sir. I'm on my way."

To a madhouse, thought Miles Perry, hanging up

the phone. Why had he agreed to supervise this con? It was going to be the longest weekend of his life. He just knew it. Of course, he knew exactly why he had agreed to run the con. It would make him very important among the area fen, gain him prestige with the national organizations, and it made him feel delightfully important, something he never felt while managing the grocery produce section at Food Lion. It was an ego trip—but it took its psychic toll.

Marion had almost been awakened by the sound of the shower, but she discovered that if she put her head under both pillows, she could ignore it enough to go on sleeping, incorporating a Tahitian waterfall into her last dream.

Jay Omega pulled back the bed covers. "Wake up, sunshine!" he said, tickling her foot. "Time to commute to fairyland."

Marion groaned. "May an orc eat you for breakfast."

Jay Omega pushed a copy of the Rubicon program under the pillow. "Lots of things to do today. No time to sleep."

"My God," she moaned, stretching and making a grab for the bedspread. "Not only do you have a Ph.D. in engineering and the ability to fix cars, you're also a morning person. Or a morning android. The possibility that you are human gets remoter all the time."

"Flattery will get you nowhere. Get up or it's the wet washcloth on your neck."

She looked at him curiously. "Are you that anxious to get to the con?"

"No. It doesn't start for another two hours. That

will give us time to eat breakfast and to visit an auto parts store I know that opens at eight. I need a master cylinder for my clutch. Then, if you insist, we can go to the con."

Marion threw a pillow. "Shut up, Android, or I'll unplug your surge protector."

Jay Omega grinned. "I think you already have."

"Really?" She sat up, smoothing her hair. "I think we have time for that."

"Too late. I've already showered." He started to rummage in his suitcase. "Hurry up, will you? I'm starving!"

Marion yawned and ambled to the bathroom. Maybe he really is an android, she thought.

In the video lounge those pulling an all-nighter were watching as the credits to *The Day the World Ended* rolled up the screen.

"Man, I knew the rain was going to kill the mutants," said Bill Fox, flipping off the television. Because of his status as a mechanical engineering major at Tech, Fox, a member of the Rubicon steering committee, was in charge of the video room.

The six people sprawled on chairs and couches throughout the room went on sleeping. Two other video junkies yawned and stretched. "I thought that was a lot scarier last time I saw it," one remarked.

"How old were you then?"

"About eight."

Joseph Bonnenberger, still in his lair in the corner, looked up to see why the sound had stopped. "Television," he said.

"Breakfast time," said Bill. "Knock off till nine. Gotta go get something to eat." He watched Bonnenberger dump his change on the end table. "Candy machines are in the hall next to the lobby, man."

"Anybody got a program handy?" asked a sleepy Star Fleet officer, uncurling out of a lounge chair.

"Yeah," said Bill. "Usual stuff starts at nine. Videos, wargames, art show, hucksters. Then at ten, there's a live-action D&D game that begins in the lobby. Real weapons strictly forbidden. And the art pro will have a seminar also at ten."

"Is Dungannon talking today?"

"One o'clock in the auditorium. Anything else you need?"

"Just a toothbrush."

"Use your finger." Bill Fox scooped up the videos and started out the door, nearly colliding with Brenda Lindenfeld in the hall.

She was still wearing her velvet gown, but her expression had softened considerably from the fierce scowl of the night before. She was escorted by a scrawny young man in a green turtleneck who walked beside her when hallway space permitted it.

Bill Fox turned back to the video lounge. "Hey! Who was that guy with Brenda Lindenfeld?"

Bonnenberger looked up from his book. Since he and Bill were alone in the lounge, he decided to venture a quip. "Her lunch," he said.

You always got more of Bonnenberger when there was no one else around.

Walter Diefenbaker hoped the registration clerk would be back from breakfast soon. He should have asked someone to bring him something from McDon-alds. Now he had a choice between peanut butter crackers from the vending machine or missing the live D&D game. Dief was not a fantasy person, but he did allow himself an occasional frivolity, and the role-playing sounded like a lark. Today his tweed jacket sported a button reading:

IS THERE REALLY A CANADA,
OR ARE ALL THOSE GUYS JUST KIDDING?

He should check with Miles, though, to see if he could be spared for the duration of the game. If one of the staff volunteers failed to show up, Miles would need someone to pitch in. Where was Miles, anyway? He hadn't been around all morning.

"Hello!" said Marion, leaning over the registration desk. She had changed her *Avengers* costume for a preppy-looking navy blazer and canvas skirt. "Jay has gone upstairs to get his books. When would you like him to set up?"

Dief shrugged. "Whenever. How long can he stand to autograph? We did want to talk to him, though. The local physicist who was going to lecture on quasars at eleven has canceled out, and we were hoping that Dr. Omega might be willing to conduct a writing seminar."

"I don't know. Surely Appin Dungannon . . ."

"Surely *not* Appin Dungannon."

"I'm not sure Jay would have much to say to a writing seminar," said Marion. "He's not very chatty about his work, and he doesn't subscribe to *Writer's*

Digest or anything like that. You can ask him, of course."

"I'll see if Miles has managed to come up with anything else. There's always the *Star Trek Bloopers* reel, I suppose."

"I'll watch the table for him if you can get him to do it. I suppose he could autograph a few books before he leaves. And sometime today we'd better let him spend some time in the computer room. The high-tech toys are his greatest joy."

Miles Perry came out of the elevator looking more harassed than ever. His rust-colored hair hung over one eyebrow in a stubborn ringlet, and he was wearing his tie at half-mast. "Here you are!" he called to Diefenbaker. "I'm thinking of enrolling in the federal witness protection program, provided they can grant me a new identity today. I want never to be seen again."

"And let Chip Livingstone run the con?" smiled Dief.

"Very funny," said the director with a sour smile. "I'm serious, Walter. This is fraying my nerves."

Dief nodded sympathetically. "More chaos?"

Miles started with the pre-dawn phone call, and summarized the rest of his hectic morning. "Just now Brian Kramer locked himself out of the wargames room, and he couldn't remember where he'd put the key."

"Did you find it?"

"Finally. After a frantic search. It was in the bag with his Diplomacy pieces. Did you hear that Dr. Zachary canceled?"

"Quasars at eleven? Yes. I was just asking Marion

if she thought Dr. Omega would do something instead."

Miles Perry shook his head. "Don't bother. You know Jack Carlton from the hucksters' room? Comic book dealer? He's agreed to try to explain the alternate Earth systems in the Superman series and how they were resolved."

Dief whistled. "In an hour?"

"Well, it's a start. Now, what are you doing on registration?"

"Calm down. Dixie went to breakfast."

"Okay. What else should I worry about?"

"Me," said Dief. "I haven't eaten."

Miles Perry pulled half a Mars bar from his jacket pocket. "With my compliments and best wishes," he said.

At ten o'clock the hotel lobby resembled an evacuation center for Sherwood Forest. A colorful crowd in homespun cloaks and rope-belted tunics milled about, discussing their player characters and speculating about the live role-playing game that was about to begin.

"I don't see why we can't use our weapons in this thing. Realism is what it's all about."

"Do you think Appin Dungannon will show up?"

Diefenbaker listened to the conversations swirling about him, but he was trying to concentrate on formulating his character. He had been assigned the part of an elf-thief, chaotic-good, with the usual agility and night vision. The other elves in the party, three giggly young women in burlap dresses, had decided to name themselves Rowan, Saffron, and Rosemary.

"And who are you going to be?" they asked him.

"Herb," said Diefenbaker.

In the center of the throng the Dungeon Master, in a monk's robe and sandals, waved his scenario and shouted for quiet. "Listen up, people!" roared Jack Larson with a most unmedieval New Jersey accent. "We're going to start now, so shut up while I read you about the quest."

He glared belligerently at the few remaining talkers, and suddenly caught sight of a familiar white-haired personage in the crowd. "Clifford Morgan! Is that you? Don't you ever learn?"

Morgan had joined the party of adventurers attired as usual in his Tratyn Runewind costume. He twirled the edge of his cloak in a bow to the Dungeon Master. "The golden Rune warrior honors you with his presence. May his skill in battle and his Druid wisdom serve you well."

"Oh, let him go," said one of the clerics. "Dungannon won't be around anyway. He's writing, remember?"

Monk Malone in his usual Dominican friar's outfit joined the group, acknowledging a flutter of applause with a modest wave. "I must be a wizard, of course," he told the Dungeon Master.

Jack Larson sighed. "I've already got a wizard."

"My apprentice," said Monk Malone smoothly. "Certainly I shall be the principal wizard in the party."

"Uh huh." Jack Larson glanced at his game plan, trying to decide how long it would be necessary to wait before letting the wererats eat the people who gave him a hard time. Jack Larson's calligraphy button said:

GOD IS DEAD,
AND I WANT HIS JOB.

When the twenty-two participants had seated themselves around the overstuffed chair, the Dungeon Master explained their mission. The human fighters were all apprentice knights in the fourteenth-century court of the king of France.

"But what about me?" asked Mona Walton. "I'm human/fighter but—a woman squire?"

Jack Larson thought fast. "Yes. Because . . . because a famous wizard has predicted that a woman warrior will someday save France, and when you asked to be trained, they were afraid to turn you away in case you turned out to be the one."

Mona nodded. "Joan of Arc. Am I?"

"No," said a Scadian. "Wrong century."

"Right. Now one of you human warriors . . ." He consulted his notes. "Gawaine . . ."

"You pronounce it *Gavin*," said the Scadian.

"Whatever. He's from Scotland. Who's Gawai—Gavin?"

One of the better-looking fourteen-year olds raised his hand. "I am."

"Okay. You're nominal leader of the group. You're the son of a clan chief, and he sent you to France to learn warfare, but you don't want to be a knight. You want to study magic. Okay?"

The boy nodded.

"Now, one day you're in your room studying your Latin when a message arrives for you from your father in Scotland." Larson paused for effect. "Someone has been stealing black horses throughout the Borders. Only black horses."

The adventurers whispered among themselves.

"So you decide that something magic and dangerous is happening. You don't know what. But you decide to go back to Scotland with some of your friends and try to find out."

"We're going to Scotland?" Tratyn Runewind applauded. Sensing their cue, the human fighters got to their feet.

"One more thing," said the Dungeon Master. "At the bottom of the letter is another note."

"What does it say?" asked Gawaine anxiously.

Jack Larson grinned at the group. "Come back when you find it."

Bill Fox, setting up "The Trouble with Tribbles" on the VCR, caught a glimpse of Walter Diefenbaker wandering down the corridor wearing the myopic lost look of Mole in *Wind in the Willows*. "Hey, Dief!" he called. "How's it going?"

Dief sighed. "I am a very stupid Scottish elf named Herb, and I am supposed to warn the adventurers to look out for 'Beans in the Road.' Whatever that means. Most of the others are searching for—not the message; they found that—a ring of Saracens, I think. Although having infidels in Scotland, even near the time of the Crusades, strikes me as being a bit far-fetched. Still, I suppose it means something sensible. The Scadians will probably know."

Bill Fox grinned. "The fantasy people are probably in their rooms thumbing through their folklore texts."

"Herb!—Yoo hoo!—Herb!"

Dief, finally realizing that he was being addressed by the name of his player character, turned to find his fellow elf Saffron waving at him from the elevator.

"Excuse me," he said to Bill Fox. "Delusion calls."

Saffron held the elevator until he arrived. "You'll never guess what I found out!" Her elfin eyes shone with excitement.

"Probably not," Dief admitted.

"The Ring of Saracens! I know what it is."

Dief remembered Bill's remark about the folklore texts. "Which book was it in?"

"None that I know of. I was right here in the elevator trying to figure out the clue . . . You know, muttering to myself, over and over, Saracen . . . Saracen . . . And this short, oldish guy got on at the third floor, and on the way down, he overheard me. He said, 'Why are you blethering about a pub in Glasgow?' "

"That's what it is? A pub in Glasgow?"

"No. Did I mention he talked funny? It turns out he's from Scotland himself."

Dief nodded. "That would be Mr. McRory."

"I guess so. Anyway, I asked him if that pub would have been around in the fourteenth century, but he said no, so I asked him what else the word *Saracen* could mean in Scotland. And he told me!"

"Well?"

"It's a ring of big stones. You know, like Stonehenge. That's what they call them in Scotland. Saracen Stones. Isn't it great that I got it?"

Diefenbaker hesitated. "I guess so, Carolyn. I mean, Saffron. But remember that you're an elf. It's the humans who have to find out what it means."

"That's okay!" said Saffron brightly. "I'm a very unusual elf. Lawful good. I can befriend a human and tip him off. I think I'll tell Gawaine. He's cute."

"Hmm. Where's everybody else?"

"Running all over the hotel, I guess. The Dungeon Master has people going everywhere looking for clues."

Appin Dungannon was pleased with his chapter. It shone on his computer screen like a bad deed in a saccharine world, and as usual he had enjoyed the thrill of finality in rereading that special chapter. He glanced at his watch. Nearly ten-thirty. His editor was due to arrive soon. In time for lunch, he hoped. Louis could always charge it to the publisher's expense account.

Suddenly he remembered that he would be addressing the entire convention at one. Damn! He hoped Louis wasn't hungry. Given a choice between a burger at rush hour and a lunch deferred, he would always choose the latter.

Pressing Home, Home, Up, Appin Dungannon scanned the chapter from the beginning, looking for typos and other lapses of concentration. Thus far he hadn't found any. His work had been pretty good this weekend, all things considered. No one had bothered him all morning. He was pleased that he had frightened the fen so thoroughly that they had left him alone.

Of course, one of them hadn't been frightened. He glanced again at the note he'd found under his door last night. Not frightened at all. But Dungannon was pleased with the overall results of his weekend. His image was intact.

He supposed he ought to get a printout made for Louis, archaic bastard that he was. As a science fiction editor, Louis would believe in six impossible things before breakfast, including a civilization of cloud beings, but you couldn't convince him that a floppy disk was as good as a manuscript. It was a pain to lug a printer around in his travels. Appin Dungannon smiled to himself: not that he ever lugged personally, of course.

He adjusted the paper feed in the printer and flipped on the machine. There was probably something ironic about creating rune sagas on a computer; he wondered what *Beowulf* would have been like, had it been word-processed. Longer, probably. He reached for a blank notecard and scribbled a memo to himself. That might make an interesting talk: the effects of technology on world perception. It had occurred to him before. Late twentieth-century people saw landscapes as a moving panorama, going by at fifty-five miles per hour. Surely this made their thinking different from the rest of humanity, who had seen landscape as a static view, like a painting. Such differences in perception probably meant that he had failed miserably at capturing the ethos of Celtic Britain, but at least he had the wit to realize it. Unlike the buffoons who thought they could live his works and still cook their dinners in a microwave. There was more to capturing the past than dressing the part. He wondered if such a lecture to a fantasy audience would be a waste of breath.

The printer was noisy, but probably no more than a television tuned to one of those mindless game shows. No one should be trying to sleep at this hour of the morning anyway. Appin Dungannon leaned back in his chair and watched the machine spit out pages of pseudo-Celtic drivel. Maybe in the next one he would have a French character named Louis confined to a leper colony near Glastonbury. Louis the Leper. It had a ring to it. He wondered if his editor would let that one go by. Tratyn Runewind goes to find someone at a leper colony near Glastonbury . . . It was the wrong period, of course. There weren't any lepers in Britain until the time of the Crusades, but he doubted if any of his readers knew that. He turned the idea over in his mind. Yes, it was interesting. One might bring in the healing wells . . . He grabbed for another notecard, and wrote down "Lepers. Glastonbury." What could he use for a working title? Books went better for him if they had names.

Appin Dungannon was still snickering at his new creation, *A Farewell to Arms*, when he heard the knock on the door.

Louis, already? Dungannon glanced at the printer. Judging by the size of the paper stack, it still had a good bit to go. With a sigh, he bent over his notecard, intent upon looking busy, and called out, "Come in! It's open."

The visitor wasn't Louis.

Appin Dungannon looked at the long hair, the medieval costume, the pseudo-Norse medallion, and then at the pistol that was leveled at his chest.

"Young man," he said. "That is an out-of-period weapon."

CHAPTER 10

LOUIS WARREN STUDIED the Rubicon program posted in the hotel lobby while he considered his options. It was now eleven twenty-nine A.M. He could either go up to Appin Dungannon's room now, and be shouted at for wasting the author's valuable time with a social call, or he could wait until a few minutes before Dungannon's scheduled one o'clock lecture, and be accused of slighting his company's top author.

As usual he wondered why he hadn't stayed in teaching, and as usual he told himself that the chairman of the English department was probably much like Appin Dungannon. At least as an editor, he could limit his encounters with the ogre to two or three times a year, instead of having to endure him more or less constantly as a faculty member. Like chest X rays, one had to give the system time to overcome the toxicity before exposing oneself to another dose.

It seemed a shame to end his stay in Washington with a visit to Appin Dungannon, but they did need the new manuscript quickly, since the withdrawal of the Maysfield novel had left a hole in their September list. Of course, Dungannon had refused to send the manuscript by courier: too expensive; too much trouble; he didn't trust the company. Louis Warren sighed. He should never have let Dungannon know that their trips to Washington coincided. Of course Dungannon would insist on personal attention. His ego required any amount of that nonsense. For one uneasy moment, Warren wondered if the author had something even more humiliating planned for their meeting. He pictured Dungannon ordering him to stay for the lecture, and then introducing him to the fannish multitude of would-be authors and instructing him to accept unsolicited manuscripts. The very idea of being deluged with several dozen incoherent Tolkien ripoffs made the editor queasy. Perhaps he should try to find a copy of the *Chronicle of Higher Education* to take back on the plane. It always featured several pages of job listings.

Deciding to get it over with, Louis Warren inquired at the front desk for Dungannon's room number. "He's expecting me," he explained to the hesitant clerk.

"Better you than me." The young man grinned. "Shall I call him and say you're on your way up?"

Warren shook his head. "One interruption is enough." Besides, he thought, advance notice would only give him more time to work on his rage.

Warren hardly noticed the assorted costumed fen who swarmed about him in the hotel. At least once a year the publisher sent him to do workshops at one of the larger cons, where he would explain to an audience of elves and Conans that the world didn't really need another book about six cloaked adventurers in search of a magic sword. And, no, he wasn't interested in the one about the Vietnam vet transported back to the time of the Visigoths, either. A variation of that one came in about once a month. Fantasy fans worked very hard on their literary creations, and seemed to have an infinite capacity for churning out pages—much greater than his capacity for reading them—but they were sadly lacking in originality; probably all that television they'd watched since infancy: formula and imitation. It was a rare young fantasy writer who managed to escape its pall.

When the elevator stopped, Louis Warren edged past two Imperial Storm Troopers, and followed the room numbers to Appin Dungannon's lair. The DO NOT DISTURB signs came as no surprise; he'd half expected barbed wire as well.

"Mr. Dungannon! Are you there? It's Louis Warren." He accompanied this announcement with a discreet and, he hoped, inoffensive tap on the door.

All was silent within.

Naturally Appin Dungannon would not bother to answer the door right away. He probably had a standard chart for how long to keep people waiting: room service five minutes, reporters eight minutes, associate editors fifteen minutes. Fans: twenty to life.

Louis Warren knocked again. "Mr. Dungannon, I'm here to pick up the manuscript." Putting his ear against the door, Louis could hear the faint clack of a printer in operation. Surely Dungannon would not leave the room with the printer going. Or perhaps he would. Warren looked at his watch. Quarter to twelve. It was perfectly possible for Dungannon to have gone to lunch, leaving it up to the editor to collect the manuscript. He supposed he ought to check, since the alternative would be to camp out in the hallway for a couple of hours, wishing pestilence and famine on Appin Dungannon, while passing Trekkies mistook him for an autograph hound.

Louis Warren tried the door handle. It wasn't locked, so he eased his way into the room, wondering whether Dungannon was present, and about to hurl a lamp at his head, or absent, and planning to have him arrested for breaking and entering. Perhaps he ought to leave a note.

The only sound in the room was the clack of the printer. Warren looked at the unmade bed, the row of bottles on the window ledge, the cowboy hat atop the computer monitor, and finally at Appin Dungannon, seated in a chair by the desk.

He looked much as usual: bulging piggy eyes, gargoyle face, unfashionably long hair. . . . The pallor was a change from his usual boozy redness, though, and the stain on his shirt was definitely not Chivas Regal. . . . Louis Warren kept staring at the body, idly wondering if he had two more wishes coming.

Finally the shock wore off a bit, and he stumbled back into the hall, nearly colliding with a tall, black-cloaked vampire. "Excuse me," murmured Louis Warren. "I wonder if you would know anything about death?"

Several minutes later, the still-dazed editor had been taken to Miles Perry and Walter Diefenbaker, who had been on their way to lunch. When he explained who he was and what he'd found, Miles Perry frantically hurried off to notify police and hotel officials, leaving a shaken Dief to cope with Louis Warren, and wondering if he were ever going to get another square meal.

"Poor, poor man!" said Dief, shaking his head. "I'm afraid that I always found him rather . . . unpleasant— probably my fault for not getting to know him better. I expect he was a rather lonely soul really. Still, I'm quite sorry he's passed on."

The editor didn't seem to be listening. Probably shock, Diefenbaker decided. One was never prepared for something like this.

"Can I get you a Coke?" murmured Dief, hoping for an excuse to seek out the vending machines. "I'm sure you must be quite shaken up."

"No, I'll be fine," said Warren vaguely. "It was a shock, that's all. And there's so much to do."

"I'm sure there must be. Had he any family?"

The editor wasn't listening. "Really, a lot of things to do. His book jacket biography will have to be rewritten, and publicity will have to design some new ads for the magazines. 'Appin Dungannon's Last Book,' something like that."

"I see."

"And I'll have to call Harlan Ellison and get him to work on a eulogy for Dungannon."

"Harlan Ellison? But I thought he hated Dungannon's work," said Dief.

Warren didn't respond, but looked over at Diefenbaker, suddenly remembering that he was there. "Is there a phone I could use?"

Walter Diefenbaker sighed. "Perhaps you ought to wait until you've talked to the police."

At one-ten P.M. most of the fen had gathered in the auditorium to hear Appin Dungannon's lecture. His lateness did not surprise them, but the absence of a stammering con official apologizing for the delay was noted as being unusual.

Jay Omega and Marion had joined the group about one-oh-five P.M., after a salad-bar lunch in the dining room, and the stragglers from the morning's role-playing game came in shortly thereafter.

"Has anybody seen Appin Dungannon?"

"He doesn't skip out on scheduled lectures, does he?"

"Nah. He has to keep getting the venom out of his system, or else he'll need dialysis."

Marion recognized the monk's robe in the row in front of her. "You were the Dungeon Master for the game this morning, weren't you? How did it go?"

"Pretty well," Jack Larson replied. "Some of them were a little slow with the clues, but they finally figured out who'd be stealing black horses in fourteenth-century Scotland."

"Who?" asked Jay Omega.

"Thomas the Rhymer," said Marion. "Right? I expect he'd need them for the Sleeping Warriors."

"Very good," said Jack Larson. "It took the group an hour and a half to come up with that. How'd you know?"

Marion smiled. "Ph.D. in folklore."

"Who are the Sleeping Warriors?" asked Jay Omega.

"I'll give you a reading list," Marion replied.

At the sound of sporadic applause they looked up at the stage to see Walter Diefenbaker making his way hesitantly to the microphone. "I just remembered you," he blurted out.

Shaking his head, he began again. "Your master of ceremonies, Miles Perry, has been detained by an emergency, and I've been asked to tell you that—" The police had not yet arrived, and he didn't really know what he was authorized to tell them. Squinting out into the audience, he saw Marion and Jay Omega giving him puzzled looks.

Diefenbaker decided on discretion; explanations could follow. "I came to tell you that our guest speaker, Appin Dungannon, is unable to be with us this afternoon due to a sudden illness—"

"Cirrhosis isn't sudden!" someone called out.

"—and so, instead of Mr. Dungannon, we will have our other guest author, Jay Omega, discuss the contemporary science fiction market with you." He motioned for Jay Omega to take the stage.

"What the hell!" hissed the substitute speaker.

"Go on!" whispered Marion. "They're obviously in a bind, so you might as well help them out. You can do it! You lecture six hours a week."

"On engineering. I've never tried to talk about writing."

"Go on, Jay! It'll be good for the book."

Jay Omega, grinning nervously, joined Dief on stage.

"What's going on?" he muttered under cover of the applause.

Diefenbaker muttered back, "Dungannon has

been murdered. Try to keep them here at least till two." He hurried away.

Jay Omega stared open-mouthed at the departing Dief until he remembered that two hundred people were staring at him from the darkened audience. He summoned up a faint smile and tried to collect his thoughts. Dungannon was dead? He couldn't have been much more than fifty. Omega wished he could say something—some expression of regret— but obviously the con people didn't want it made public. He felt a twinge of guilt for having envied Dungannon his celebrity as a writer.

Jay Omega adjusted the microphone stand a few inches upward to accommodate the height difference. "Good afternoon," he said to the audience. "I'm sure I won't be as helpful as Appin Dungannon would have been, but I'll do my best. As you know, I write hard science fiction, so I may not be much help to you aspiring fantasy writers, although I will say that if you plan to write about things like the Sleeping Warriors, a doctorate in folklore wouldn't hurt. Now before I talk about my own work, does anyone have any questions?"

A student in the third row raised his hand. "Do you make more money from your first novel or from teaching engineering?"

Marion sighed. "Now there's a fantasy for you!"

Miles Perry did not think that things boded well for Rubicon. "If You Never Attend Another SF Convention in Your Life: Go to Rubicon. —They'll Guarantee It!" He could imagine the snide comments in 'zines across the country. Meanwhile, he was waiting for the police officers to finish their work in Dungannon's room. He said he'd be available for questioning. At least he didn't have to worry about an alibi: never having had a moment's peace all morning ought to provide one nonstop.

He found that he was sweating profusely and, alert to appearances, he took out his handkerchief to mop his brow. A real murder! He had half hoped that the police would invite him up to the room, so that he could watch the photographing and the gathering of evidence. Would they put a chalk outline where the body had been? But upon reflection he decided that the time to himself might be more valuable in his present state of agitation. What did one do when the special guest expired at the con? Canceling the banquet was out of the question. He supposed it ought to be a subdued affair, in memory of the deceased.

Someone was sure to suggest a chorus of "Ding Dong! The Witch is Dead!" That had to be quashed at the outset. Decorum would be the watchword. He hoped the murderer wouldn't turn out to be someone else famous, like Jay Omega. That would be too much notoriety for any con.

"Mr. Perry? We're ready to ask you a few questions now." Lt. Thomas Ayhan, with a gray crewcut and a rumpled brown suit, was easily the most distinguished person at the con. Miles thought he looked more like a bank vice-president than a policeman, and one made him as uneasy as the other. Ayhan smiled reassuringly and pulled out a little blue notebook. "Oh, before we begin, I need to ask you: was the deceased a Roman Catholic, by any chance?"

Miles Perry stared. "I very much doubt it," he said. "Why?"

"Well, we wondered. There was a priest asking for admittance to the room, and I thought he might want to administer the last rites."

"Hmm. Long black robe with a rope belt? Skinny guy with a beard?"

Lt. Ayhan nodded.

"Don't let him in. That's Monk Malone. He's not a priest; he's a fan."

"One of the members of your convention, then?"

"Yes. But we haven't told anybody that Dungannon is dead, so how did he know?"

"We're not all that inconspicuous," smiled Ayhan. "I think he must have seen us come in, and followed to see what was going on."

"If he knows, it'll be all over the hotel soon," said Miles.

Louis Warren had missed his plane, but that was the least of his worries. Sometime during his frantic review of things to be done, it suddenly occurred to him that the manuscript he had come for was lying in a room that was now sealed and guarded by the police department. He rushed to the door of the conference room, but unable to think of anything he could actually do about the situation, he sat down and tried to think up arguments for getting the detectives to return the manuscript. Ought he to call the legal department?

He looked up as Diefenbaker came in, carrying a couple of Cokes. "I got Jay Omega to take over the lecture," he said, puffing a little from the unaccustomed haste. "Have the police spoken to you yet?"

"No. I suppose they'll insist on it, since I found the body, but there's really nothing I can tell them."

"Do you know who would have wanted to kill him?" asked Dief.

"Sure. Get a copy of the *Directory of American Poets and Fiction Writers* and start with A. You could have raffled off chances to kill Appin Dungannon."

Diefenbaker thought about last night's performance at the costume competition. "He didn't seem to mind making enemies," he conceded.

"No. He had quite a gift for it," Warren agreed, sipping his drink.

"I suppose your company will miss a best-selling author, though."

"They might, but I won't," said the editor. "Imagine being able to edit a Tratyn Runewind book without having to wrangle over every semicolon, or justify every deleted adjective. It's going to be wonderful!"

"I suppose a woman could have shot him," said Diefenbaker thoughtfully. "Didn't he have an ex-wife?"

"Yes. Doubleday is bringing out her book this spring: *Beauty and the Beast: A Marriage Made in Munchkinland*. If it's still in galleys, they'll probably want to do a rewrite on her last chapter."

"You don't think she's in town, do you?"

"She lives in California. She'll be easy to find. Check the talk-show circuit. I don't think she did it; no motive, really. The same goes for all the relatives. Alive, they got all the money they needed. But

Dungannon stipulated that, upon his death, the estate would go to the Scottish Archaeological Society. Everybody knows that, especially the ex-wife. Still," he mused, "it would make great publicity for the book if she did! I wonder who has the paperback rights?"

Jay Omega had stressed the value of reading to improve one's writing style; he had recommended a computer for ease of corrections; and he had urged them to write what they knew, insisting that in today's world of high technology, a knowledge of science could not be faked.

The audience of would-be writers had countered with questions about publisher's advances, agents' percentages, and movie rights. Jay Omega, whose experience in all of these was limited, advised them to hold such questions until after the rewrite of the first draft.

"Any more questions?" he asked, trying to sound cheerful.

A clean-cut young man in a suit stood up. "I am interested in becoming a writer," he said, with the unctuous charm of a business major. "And I was wondering about this business of setting up an office in your home in which to write. I know it can't double as a guest room, but I was wondering whether you can deduct the entire cost of your computer and office furniture in the first year, or if you have to spread it out over several years. And also, can you begin to deduct depreciation on the equipment in the year of purchase?"

Jay Omega, who doubted that his royalties would

ever equal his advance for *Bimbos*, blinked at the questioner. He hadn't expected to see a yellow spotted tie in this crowd. "Well . . ." he said at last, "I think that depends. Not all writers bother with home offices . . ."

"Since most of them couldn't afford the furniture," muttered Marion.

"What have you written?" Jay Omega asked the young man.

"I haven't written anything," came the reply. "I'm sure I could, but I wanted to get all the business aspects straight before I became a professional."

Jay Omega was beginning to understand why Appin Dungannon threw folding chairs. He wondered how to answer someone who thought of writing as just another business, and then he remembered a line that might apply. "Uh . . . well . . . it's like this," he stammered. "Being a professional writer is a lot like being a hooker. You'd better find out if you're any good at it before you start charging for it."

Marion giggled to herself. If he doesn't stop quoting me, I'll charge him for speech-writing, she thought.

The rest of the audience was still snickering appreciatively when Monk Malone mounted the steps to the stage. He was still wearing his black friar's habit, and beneath the dark, matted hair, his solemn face seemed to burn with purpose. Probably wants to start a children's crusade, thought Jay Omega.

"Excuse me, Mr. Omega," he said with ecclesiastical dignity. "I must make an announcement."

"I don't think—"

Monk Malone commandeered the microphone. Raising both hands as if he were offering an invocation, he called out, "I have an announcement of the utmost gravity!"

"How many G's?" yelled a NASA freak.

Monk Malone silenced him with a smoldering stare.

"The Force is with us in the person of its darkest horseman. You may see it as a judgment, or as the caprice of the goddess Weird, but it has come to pass. I must now inform you that Appin Dungannon is no more."

Marion's jaw dropped. For once, she found herself speechless.

Jay Omega clutched the lectern and looked down at his shoes, half in embarrassment, half with genuine regret.

For a stunned second no one moved. Then a voice near the back row blurted out, "Holy shit!" and the audience sprang to life.

"Cut down in the flower of his creativity . . ." Monk Malone was saying.

"What was it? Heart attack?"

"I saw some cops in the lobby!" someone called out. "I figured it was a disturbing-the-peace rap."

"Cops! —Was he murdered?"

Suddenly a clarion voice rang out like a battle cry above the babble. "The hucksters' room! While we still can!"

In the row in front of her, Jack Larson snatched up his cloak and prepared to join the stampede to the door. Marion leaned over and touched his arm. "The hucksters' room?" she echoed. "What does that have to do with Appin Dungannon's being murdered?"

The Dungeon Master smiled at her. "Not a thing," he replied. "But life goes on. And now autographed copies of Appin Dungannon's books are worth triple what they were five minutes ago."

CHAPTER 11

MILES PERRY DIDN'T think that homicide detectives ought to giggle while investigating a murder. Still, he supposed it was better than a granite-faced Joe Friday look that radiated suspicion. Beneath his salt-and-pepper crew cut, Lt. Ayhan reddened with suppressed chuckles. Tears appeared at the corners of his eyes, and he kept taking deep breaths that would almost turn into whoops.

"I'm glad he wasn't stabbed with a broadsword," he managed to say. "I'd hate to have to book an elf!"

"Elves use shortswords," said Miles Perry.

Ayhan continued to chuckle. "Or pixie dust poisoning. That would have been a toughie!"

Miles endeavored to look stern. "We are seriously concerned over Mr. Dungannon's death, both personally and as a reflection on the integrity of our convention," he said stiffly.

Ayhan dabbed at his eyes. "Sorry," he said cheerfully. "After years of winos with their heads bashed in, and a slew of unpremeditated bar brawls, this does make a change. The captain asks me, 'So who do you have for suspects?' and I say, 'Dopey, Bashful,

126

and Doc!' " He shook his head. "This is one for the memoirs."

"I trust the murderer will turn out to be someone sufficiently colorful," said Miles politely.

"No matter," said Ayhan. "We'll get him. People watch too much TV these days. They think if they wipe off the fingerprints and ditch the murder weapon, they're safe. Nah. We got all kinds of fancy lab tests. Did you know that firing a pistol leaves a minute powder residue on your hand? True. All we need are a few likely suspects. Now if this was one of them Mystery Writers of America conventions, I might be worried. Those folks are all hopped up on police procedure, but here? Not to worry. Twelve hours of legwork and a little questioning, and it'll be a wrap."

"It will be all right to go ahead with the con, won't it?" asked Miles with a worried frown. "We have a banquet tonight that can't be canceled, and we couldn't afford to give refunds."

Lt. Ayhan considered it. "I don't see why not," he said. "It'll keep everybody in one place, which will be nice from our point of view. My people will probably be finished with the death scene soon anyhow. The hotel people always want the room back post haste. Shocking, isn't it?"

"I guess so. Will you want to question everybody? They're all in the auditorium now. I could make an announcement."

Ayhan grimaced and looked at the ceiling. "Everybody?" he sighed. "All the Merry Men? That would take forever; waste of time. Why don't you tell me what the victim has been up to here? Any quarrels? Anybody have a grudge against him?"

Miles Perry's lips twitched. "And that's going to narrow it down?" As quickly as he could, he described Appin Dungannon's general outrageousness, from the Yorkie bars to the breakfast croissants, hitting all the tantrums in between.

Lt. Ayhan noted it all very carefully in his little blue book. "So if annoyance is a motive, you could be in the suspect semifinals, right?"

"If you could kill by mental telepathy, I'd probably be guilty, but physically I wouldn't lift a finger toward anybody."

Ayhan glanced up at Miles Perry's comfortable bulk. Physically he probably lifted as little as possible, the detective was thinking. "So he insulted everybody last night, in a general way? How about this kid he threw chairs at? What's his name? Morgan?"

"Oh, he wasn't angry about that," Miles assured him. "Clifford Morgan was thrilled to have drawn so much attention from an Eminent Pro. He'll be famous now."

"Famous? How? He's going to sue?"

"No. I mean in fandom. People will write up stories in fan magazines describing the incident, and it will become part of fannish history. Some cons may pay Cliff's way now, just to have him on hand to tell the tale."

Ayhan frowned. "Are there any drugs floating around this thing?"

"Of course not!" gasped Miles, indignant. "The fen are not into drugs, except maybe the old ones, left over from the Sixties. You don't have to worry about that."

"I wasn't worried," said Ayhan. "I understand drugs. Drug killings are straightforward. All this elf-and-image stuff is a real bear, though. But I've heard of it. My kid, when he was in junior high, got into a D&D group for a while. I think he was a warrior."

Miles Perry looked interested. "Your son is a fan?"

"Nah. He was. But then he got to tenth grade, and discovered girls and j.v. football. I guess you could say he outgrew it. He's at Wake Forest now, in pre-law. Now, did Mr. Dungannon attend the con by himself? No wife, girlfriend, agent?"

"He was alone. He is or at least *was* married. He was divorced a few years ago. She is writing a book about her life with him, and we had hoped to have her as a guest at one of our future cons."

"Hmmm, who did he spend time with while he was here?"

Miles Perry thought about it. "When he wasn't sort of being available—you know, for autographs and that sort of thing—he was in his room finishing his book. I guess the only people who really saw much of him were at dinner last night."

"Ah! I'll start with them." He flourished his notepad. "Their names?"

"Uh, Walter Diefenbaker—you've met him. Jay Omega, he's also a guest author. Marion Farley, she's a professor who teaches science fiction, and is also Jay's—what do they say nowadays—'significant other'—"

"S-i-g-n-i-f-i-c-a-n-t O-t-h-e-r," wrote Ayhan.

"—and, er, of course," clucked Miles guiltily, "myself."

"Oh?" Ayhan raised an eyebrow, and scribbled furiously.

Miles labored to produce an innocent smile.

There was a tap on the door, and Bill Fox appeared. "Excuse me, folks, but I thought you'd like to know that Monk Malone just announced to the whole auditorium that Dungannon is dead."

Miles Perry gasped. "Was there a panic? Are people leaving?"

Bill shook his head. "They're all in the hucksters' room, cornering the market on signed copies of Dungannon's work. That's free enterprise for you."

Bill Fox lingered at the door. "One more thing," he said. "That publisher guy who came to see Dungannon is real anxious to talk to the police. I promised I'd pass the word along."

Lt. Ayhan shrugged. "Somebody wants to see me? It'll make a nice change. Okay, I'll talk to him. When you see the college professor, tell him I'd like to talk to him, okay?"

With a wave of his blue notebook, the lieutenant was gone. Miles Perry frowned. Murder was so complicated ... and incriminating. Apart from which he had forgotten to ask Ayhan what he should say to reporters should any appear. He pulled out a rumpled Rubicon program and began to scribble notes.

Louis Warren was a little embarrassed to have a police detective catch him reading the *Star Trek Officers Manual*, but it had been a tedious wait since

Diefenbaker had wandered off to supervise the con activities. Thrusting the telltale volume under a sofa cushion, he sprang up to greet the officer, hand outstretched.

Lt. Ayhan responded with the cordial reserve one usually keeps for used car salesmen and unhousebroken puppies. "Do sit down, Mr. Warren. Would you show me some identification, please?"

The editor fished out his wallet and handed it over to the lieutenant, hoping that he was projecting an aura of candor and a total willingness to help the police.

"New York driver's license. You're a brave one. Health club. Very good. My wife keeps after me to join one of those. She says it's either that, or come to aerobics with her." Ayhan flipped another card, and looked up inquiringly at Warren. "Lt. Colonel in the Time Police?"

Warren reddened. "That's just a joke. The publisher sends me to a lot of cons, and at one of them, these guys were making photo I.D. cards for different things. Vulcan Science Academy Student I.D.; U.N.C.L.E. Personnel Badge. I keep it around for a joke."

"Too bad," said Ayhan with a straight face. "I was hoping you could go back to your squad room and tell me how the case was solved. Oh, well. Let's talk about Appin Dungannon."

"He was murdered, wasn't he?"

"Looks that way. Don't tell the *Enquirer* till the autopsy report comes through, though, okay? Now, what can you tell me about it?"

As he had rehearsed it during his long wait, Louis

Warren explained his reason for coming to the con, but with less emphasis on his dread of meeting the author. "The door was ajar when I went in, and the printer was going. He was dead in the chair. I didn't touch him. I didn't touch anything. At least, I don't think I did. Maybe I did. Did I?"

"We'll print you," smiled Ayhan. "And I'll get back to you on that question. So you had just arrived at the hotel at approximately eleven thirty A.M.?"

"Yes. And I didn't see ... Yes, I did. Going down the hall toward the room, I passed two Imperial Stormtroopers, and when I came out I ran into Dracula."

Lt. Ayhan sighed. "I love this case."

The windows in the Patrick Henry Nook were shrouded in mourning, and the chandelier overhead was on *dim*. It seemed appropriate. At least two of the four people convened to cope with the death of Appin Dungannon were torn between grief and panic. After all, the con must go on, but what ought to be the proper atmosphere? Miles Perry spread out his grubby Rubicon program on the coffee table in front of Marion, Jay, and Walter Diefenbaker. "The police say it's okay to continue the con—"

Jay Omega stood up. "The Lieutenant seems very bright. I have no doubt he will solve the crime before the weekend is up. Now, if you have no further need of me, I've been meaning to stop by the computer room . . ."

Miles Perry looked stricken. "You're leaving?— Oh, please don't! The rest of the committee is all over the place trying to keep things under control, and I don't want to make all the decisions by myself."

"It would be very kind of you to stay," said Diefenbaker. "If we wouldn't be imposing on you too much."

Jay looked at Marion and shrugged. "I don't mind, if you really think we'd be of any use to you. I don't know anything about cons, though."

"He chaired the Engineering Health and Safety Conference last year, though," Marion offered.

"Splendid!" cried Dief. "I know you'll be ever so sensible and organized."

Jay Omega sighed and sat down. "I'll see what I can do. You say the police have given you permission to continue the conference?"

"What about the hotel people?" asked Marion.

"Yes. I spoke to them first," said Miles. "They're all for business as usual. The less disruption there is involved, the better they can weather the publicity. They don't want the word *murder* spread around too much, by the way."

Diefenbaker nodded. "So we carry on, with certain modifications?"

"Right. I think the banquet ought to be in Appin Dungannon's honor. We could get somebody to do a tribute to him." He looked hopefully at Jay Omega.

" 'I come to bury Caesar, not praise him,' " murmured Marion.

Jay Omega divided his sour look between her and Miles Perry. "Look," he said, "I'm very sorry that Dungannon is dead, but I didn't know the man, and didn't particularly like what I saw. And besides that, I never read any of his books."

"You know who would be the logical person to eulogize him?" said Diefenbaker helpfully. "Harlan Ellison!"

Miles Perry looked at him as if he had lost his mind. "We can't afford Harlan Ellison."

"Oh," said Dief, deflated. Then he said, "What about Clifford Morgan? The greatest Dungannon fan of all? Who's read everything three times? Who lives it, for God's sake!"

Marion blinked. "Tratyn Runewind?"

Dief nodded. "He lives and breathes Dungannon. If he's not too devastated by the series ending to do it, he'd be perfect!"

"But Appin Dungannon hated Clifford Morgan!" said Jay Omega. "He threw folding chairs at him!"

Marion nodded. "It doesn't seem like a very respectful tribute. I'd be afraid he'd haunt us!"

Miles Perry had thought it over. "Well . . ." he said at last. "I think Dr. Omega would be a more distinguished speaker, but if he won't do it, we'll just have to do the best we can." He sighed. "If you can get Morgan to do it, Walter, I have no objection."

"I think Morgan will be sincere," said Dief. "I'll impress upon him that it's a solemn occasion. Imitation is supposed to be the sincerest form of flattery, so Cliff should be the most genuine mourner there.— Well, that's settled. What else needs to be changed?"

"Dungannon's last appearance. On Sunday morning he had agreed to act as Dungeon Master for an exhibition game featuring Tratyn Runewind."

"He was going to let somebody play Tratyn Runewind?" gasped Marion.

"No. Runewind will be a non-player character

controlled by the DM. The participants just get to accompany him on an adventure." Miles looked again at Jay Omega.

"I'm already signed up to play," said Diefenbaker.

Miles Perry sighed. "I have to see that the art auction gets set up. I'll have to be in and out."

Marion turned to Jay Omega. "It isn't very difficult," she said coaxingly. "I can show you all the basic things. Look at it as a chance to play God."

Jay Omega glowered at the three pleading faces before him. "Oh, all right. But don't blame me if I make a mess of it."

Louis Warren appeared at the door, looking as if he were in pursuit of the Holy Grail. He was followed by Lt. Ayhan, who looked considerably pained.

"Does anyone know anything about computers?" Louis asked feverishly.

With a straight face, Jay Omega raised his hand.

"He's designed a few," said Marion.

"Oh. I need someone to help me with a discus."

"A disk!" said Miles, Dief, and Jay Omega in unison.

"Whatever. I've explained to the lieutenant that my company absolutely has to have that manuscript now . . ."

His voice was suddenly shrill.

". . . or we will sue Dungannon's estate for return of the advance." Noticing Ayhan's raised eyebrows, Louis added defensively, "We *do* have a deadline to meet."

"Must be a pretty valuable manuscript," mused Ayhan.

"The manuscript is worth very little without the

contract," said Louis wearily, as if explaining the concept of electricity to a child. "The ex-wife, the distant relatives, the mysterious fellow in a jeep in the desert who may have picked him up hitchhiking . . . Lieutenant, they have nothing, nothing to gain. Dungannon left all of his money and rights to the Scottish Archaeological Society. Everybody knows that."

"Now," said Ayhan, "we're getting somewhere." He patiently logged another suspect on his notepad. "And who are they—or it?" he asked, not really expecting a comprehensible reply.

"Scottish history-diggers," said Louis indifferently. "Big on excavation work. Dungannon was very keen on Celtic history. No doubt they'll be pleased to receive this windfall a few years ahead of schedule—"

"Hmmm," said Ayhan, in his best speculative manner.

"—Besides," continued Louis, "Dungannon always said he liked dead people better than live ones."

"He should be ecstatic now, then," Lt. Ayhan remarked.

"So they're going to let you take the manuscript?" asked Marion.

"No way," said Ayhan.

"No," the editor admitted. "Everything in that room is evidence in the case. In case of fingerprints, or whatever."

"Policy," said Ayhan calmly.

"But I've persuaded him to let me make a copy of the disk on which the book is written."

"Correction," said Ayhan. "Under my supervision, you can get a reputable person to make a copy of the disk, provided that you obtain the second disk from a source other than the room containing the deceased."

"So all you want is for somebody to make a backup copy of a floppy disk?" said Jay Omega.

The editor nodded. "Can you do that?"

"I could do that," said Marion.

Lt. Ayhan smiled at her. "It's a handsome offer, ma'am, but we'll let the professor do it, since he has the Ph.D. and all."

Jay Omega smiled wickedly at Dr. Marion Farley. "Yes, Marion, better leave it to me, since I have the Ph.D."

"Later," said Marion between clenched teeth.

"What do you need to do this?" asked Ayhan.

Jay Omega turned to Diefenbaker. "Go to the high-tech room and ask Joel Schumann to bring me a couple of blank disks and the *Diskcopy* program." He turned to Lt. Ayhan. "Dungannon's machine is PC-compatible, isn't it?"

The detective shrugged. "For all I know, it could run on kryptonite."

Dungannon's body had been removed, but several uniformed officers were still in the room examining the deceased's personal effects and taking photographs.

Jay Omega could see no sign of a struggle, and no traces of blood in the bland modern cubicle. Dungannon's suitcase lay open on the chair, and his computer and printer occupied most of the desk space. Omega was relieved to see that it was a Sanyo portable, about 90% IBM compatible. He was afraid that Dungannon might have used some sort of mini-machine that took microdiskettes; they'd have needed a scavenger hunt to round some of those up. He was glad the regular floppies from the high-tech room would work.

"Good afternoon, gentlemen," said Lt. Ayhan to his troops. "Have we solved the case yet?"

One of the officers shook his head. "Give us a few more minutes," he grinned.

"I came back to do my good deed for the day," the lieutenant announced. "These fellows want to make a copy of the disk that Mr. Dungannon's book is on. And I said that under my careful supervision, they may do so. Have you dusted it for prints yet?"

Jay Omega winced at this suggestion.

The uniformed cop favored Ayhan with a pitying smile. "Lucky for them we didn't, Lieutenant. Rafferty tried it on a larceny case a couple of months ago, and it wrecked the disk."

"It wouldn't do the computer any good, either," Jay Omega observed. "Those little grains of powder would scratch both the disk and the reader head."

Ayhan eased himself down on the edge of the bed. "Do any of you whiz kids have any bright ideas?"

"Sure," said his grinning subordinate. "We're going to do just what they want to do. Make a copy, and then dust the original."

"It'll be an exact copy?" asked Ayhan.

"Yes," said Jay Omega. "It'll copy all forty tracks on both sides."

"The fingerprints, too?" asked Ayhan.

Jay Omega took a deep breath, and prepared to launch into a disk lecture.

"He's putting you on," said the uniformed cop. "Here's the disk. Have you got a blank one?"

Jay Omega looked up just as Joel Schumann arrived at the open door. "I brought the disks, Dr. Mega!" he called out.

"Here they are now," said Omega.

The photographer waved Joel through.

Joel and the uniformed cop grinned at the solemnity with which Jay Omega sat down to carry out this simple computer task. He inserted the DOS disk in drive A, and reached for Dungannon's master disk, but Ayhan, holding one corner with a handkerchief, signaled that he would do it himself. Finally the computer was ready to copy: master disk in A; blank disk in B.

"You brought an extra disk?" asked Ayhan.

Joel handed him one.

"Good. Consider this our fee for the favor. Another copy, please."

Two minutes and a series of clicks later, Jay Omega handed the copies to Ayhan and Louis Warren. He pointed to drive A. "You can take it out now," he told the young policeman. "Just make sure nobody tries to put it back in a computer after that."

Louis Warren held his disk gingerly between thumb and forefinger. "How do I get this on paper to give to an editor?" he asked.

Joel Schumann shrugged. "The high-tech room's IBM doesn't have a printer. You can read it on a screen there, though."

"Read it!?" Louis drew back in horror.

"You know, check to make sure it's all there—" said Joel soothingly.

"Oh," said Louis, still dubious. Joel smiled at the editor's expression of distaste and suspicion; he'd often seen that reaction in people over thirty being confronted with new technology. "Come on," he said, leading Louis away. "I'll set it up for you."

Ayhan handed his copy of the disk to the young officer. "Anything else interesting?"

Jay Omega smiled at the note of triumph in the young guy's voice.

"We found this in the wastebasket, sir."

The Lieutenant unrolled the crumpled piece of paper and studied the elegant, black calligraphy of the message:

APPIN DUNGANNON:
  You are a tiny, insufferable primadonna, and a blight on the face of fandom. You are a vain, embittered old hack who ought to give up public appearances and spend the time going to charm school ... or reading Anne McCaffrey. Either would improve you immeasurably. If you cannot bring some measure of joy and inspiration to the world you touch, then you ought to die and let the sparrows have your share of the oxygen.

After reading it twice, Ayhan glanced at the officer. "Dusted?" An affirmative nod. The lieutenant passed the paper to Jay Omega. "What do you think?"

Omega ran his finger over the page, squinted at the calligraphy, and finally said "Macintosh."

The younger cop nodded. "That's what I thought."

Ayhan whipped out his blue notebook. "Macintosh? Description? What's his first name?"

Jay Omega shrugged. "Apple?"

"London Font," said the young cop.

"I make it eighteen point."

Ayhan stopped writing. "Somebody's babbling," he announced. "Have you called in a handwriting expert?"

Jay Omega handed him back the note. "You don't need a handwriting expert," he explained gently. "This is a computer-generated document. We think it was done on a Macintosh in calligraphy script."

"So how do we find out who wrote it? Do we know who owns one of these things?"

"Well," said Jay Omega. "There's a Macintosh with a printer in the high-tech display room downstairs. My guess is that it was done there. If so, maybe Joel could tell you who used it."

"The kid that just left?" Ayhan motioned to the young cop. "Go talk to him, Simmons. Since you speak the language."

"I guess you got your first real clue," said Jay Omega, trying to be soothing.

"Yeah," growled Ayhan. "And the suspect is a fifty-pound hunk of plastic named Macintosh. I love this case."

CHAPTER 12

THE RUBICON BANQUET and Costume Ball began promptly at seven in the main ballroom of the hotel, which had been decorated for the occasion with streamers and SF movie posters. The speakers' table was set beneath a vintage *Thief of Bagdad* poster, and sported centerpieces of yellow candles and blue Tribbles, arranged in small clumps around handfuls of grain. The second chair to the left of the podium was conspicuously empty.

At the long banquet tables perpendicular to the main one, an assortment of medieval dignitaries and extraterrestrials sipped grapefruit punch (listed on the menu as Pangalactic Gargleblaster), and exchanged the latest rumors about the murder of Appin Dungannon. Since Lt. Ayhan had spent a long and tedious afternoon interviewing a cross-section of Rubicon participants, many of them had a good idea how the investigation was going, and what matters were likely to interest the police.

"Did you mention the costume contest?"

"Of course! If you didn't, they'd think you were suspicious! But did you tell them how he ruined Douglas's books with a Tolkien signature?"

"I hear Douglas told them he was glad someone had iced Dungannon, when they questioned him."

"Did they ask you about a note?"

"Yeah. And a lot of funny computer questions, too."

"Did somebody steal Dungannon's computer?"

"I heard he threw it at the murderer. Is this punch alcoholic?"

At the elevated speakers' table, above rabble and rumors and to the right of Miles Perry and the empty chair, sat Marion, sandwiched between Jay Omega and Walter Diefenbaker. The other side of the podium was reserved for the guest artist, three Rubicon board members, and the chief mourner: Clifford Morgan, a.k.a. Tratyn Runewind. Of the honored guests only a woman board member and Morgan/Runewind had appeared in costume. Dief wore his Canadian formal attire, a brown turtleneck and tweed blazer with maple-leaf lapel pin; the other men wore suits and ties. Marion had decided to be an elegant Mrs. Peel in green watered silk and pearls, but she kept the Sixties hairstyle as a tribute to her heroine.

"What is that music?" she whispered to Diefenbaker.

"Schubert. 'Death and the Maiden.' We were going to use *Star Wars* soundtrack albums, but Miles thought that this would be more fitting under the circumstances."

"Better than 'Happy Days Are Here Again,' " Marion conceded. "I'm sure somebody suggested that."

Jay Omega sipped his Gargleblaster. "I don't have to say anything formal, do I?" he asked Miles Perry.

"Not a speech," Miles promised. "But I'll introduce you later, and you can stand up."

Jay nodded toward the audience. "Are you going to introduce him, too?"

"Who?"

"Lt. Ayhan. He's sitting at that table on the left."

After an invocation by a board member directed to the Entity Who Engineered the Universe, a visibly moved Miles Perry took the podium. "Tonight is a more solemn occasion than we had meant it to be," he stammered, trying not to stare in Lt. Ayhan's direction. "At this year's Rubicon we wanted to honor one of the giants of fantasy literature—"

Several people in the audience snickered.

"A writer whose stature—"

Miles Perry reddened and pawed at his notes. "Unfortunately, Appin Dungannon is not able to be with us tonight . . ."

"Unfortunately?" called a heckler.

People began to chant "The Monkey's Paw!"

Against his better judgment, Miles glanced at Lt. Ayhan. Blast the man! He was smiling again! "Our program designed to honor Appin Dungannon, creator of the Tratyn Runewind series, has instead become a tribute to his memory. We ask that amid the festivities you keep within you a solemn remembrance of Appin Dungannon . . . a shining star in the annals of fantasy!"

Someone kicked over a folding chair.

Further speeches were not scheduled until after

dinner, by which time Miles hoped that the hilarity would have worn itself out. He ate his tepid chicken with a grim expression suggesting that he could hear it pleading for mercy. For once he hoped there weren't any journalists present; the mood of facetiousness thus far exhibited at the banquet would show them in a very bad light if reported in cold newsprint.

Lt. Ayhan had decided that as long as he had to do some questioning at the con, he might as well observe things at the banquet—when all the cracked eggs were in one basket. He was seated now across from a desperately plain young man in a brown polyester leisure suit, and a courting couple who reminded him of Kermit the Frog and Miss Piggy. He had planned to say that he liked a good science fiction novel now and then, if anyone had asked why he was there, but so far no one had taken any notice of him at all. The people he had questioned were seated at other tables. Ayhan decided that he would just listen to the general discussions, and if that proved unhelpful, he might try a few conversational gambits of his own.

"Pass the salt," said the leisure suit, whose name tag identified him as J. Bonnenberger.

Ayhan handed him the salt shaker, but before he could venture a get-acquainted remark, Bonnenberger turned to the "Kermit" kid with the turtleneck and medallion. "So who do you think killed McAfee?"

Ayhan's fork froze in midair. Who was McAfee?

"Terrorists, I guess," shrugged Richard Faber.

"My organization doesn't have any plastic explosives. We can't afford them yet."

"I think he was a double agent, anyway, so it's probably none of my business who killed him. Unless he still had the microchip on him, of course. We want that."

Ayhan's hand itched for his blue notebook. He might have to call in the NSA on this one.

"So, if he was a double agent, Bonnenberger, who do you think he was working for?" asked Faber.

"Probably the KGB. And if that was the case, then the hit was only made to *look* like a terrorist attack, to divert suspicion from the real power-brokers." Bonnenberger's last remark was somewhat garbled by the mouthful of lettuce impairing his consonant-formation. Dribbles of salad ran down each side of his mouth like a thousand-island Fu Manchu.

"Okay," nodded Faber, unaffected by his comrade's table manners. "So you think it was the Girl Scouts."

"Definitely," Bonnenberger managed to say.

"Okay. Then it was probably O.O. Wolfe. He'd have access to explosives at Fort Belvoir, and he has a high skill rating in demolitions. The Girl Scouts have nuclear capability now, too. Did you know that?"

"What are you talking about?" demanded Lt. Ayhan, who felt that he would explode if he didn't ask.

His table partners looked at him with faint surprise at such rude inquisitiveness from a stranger. The fat girl, eager to show off her limited supply of knowledge, explained. "They're in a TSR game called

Top Secret. It's sort of like D&D, but it deals with spies and secret organizations. You get characters to control, and your organization assigns you a mission. . . ."

Lt. Ayhan stopped listening, and went back to his chicken. He supposed he ought to see if Miles Perry could help him find one of the con guests who had been mentioned as a vehement critic of Dungannon. Some kid named Chip Livingstone. Truly elusive. Half a dozen people had showed him mimeographed newsletters containing criticisms of Dungannon, all signed *Chip Livingstone*. But he couldn't get a decent make on the guy. White male, early twenties—that was ninety percent of the con. And the guy wasn't on the hotel register, either. Hmmm. Also true of half the people at the con. Everybody seemed to be sleeping on couches, or six to a room. If Ayhan wasn't in Homicide, he could have a field day writing up misdemeanors. But he had put the word out to find Chip Livingstone and sooner or later he would turn up.

So far, though, zilch. Probably afraid to. Half the people Ayhan had talked to had mentioned this guy as an enemy of Dungannon. Maybe that was a bit obvious for a murder suspect, but in Ayhan's opinion, most murderers were obvious. And if the guy was innocent, where was he? Pulling out his notebook, he scribbled a note to Miles Perry, finishing it just as the waiter appeared to refill his iced tea.

"Could you give this to the gentleman sitting next to the speaker's stand?" he asked the waiter.

Faber and Bonnenberger glowered suspiciously

as the white-coated waiter glided away with the
note. Suppose the old guy with the crew cut was an
agent for the Girl Scouts? You couldn't trust anybody these days.

When Miles Perry unfolded the note from Ayhan,
he lost all interest in his second piece of pecan pie.
Two minutes from now he was due at the podium
again to introduce Clifford Morgan for the memorial
speech. He wondered if he ought to make an
announcement first. Probably so. Gumming up a
murder investigation could probably put you in
prison right along with the murderer. With a sigh
and the certain knowledge that the Force was not
with him, Miles Perry stood up and faced the mob.

"Fellow fen . . ." He looked again at the note. On
second thought, why not wait until after the eulogy?
He didn't want to upstage Morgan's big moment,
and besides, he needed time to figure out what to
say. Should he warn anyone? "As you know, our
guest speaker tonight was to have been Appin Dungannon, so it is only fitting under the circumstances
that we offer instead a tribute to that gifted writer
by one of his greatest fans. If imitation is the sincerest form of flattery, then Clifford Morgan's admiration of Dungannon knows no bounds. In the
persona of Tratyn Runewind, ladies and gentlemen,
I give you Clifford Morgan."

With a swirl of his blue satin cloak (for formal
occasions), the white-maned Tratyn Runewind
bowed to Miles Perry, and fixed the audience with a
solemn stare. "Men say there shall be no more
sagas," he intoned in a booming voice suggesting

John Wayne's portrayal of Genghis Khan. "But as the pen is mightier than the sword, so is the legend hardier than the scop. Appin Dungannon has died, but Tratyn Runewind is a child of the gods, and he will live forever. . . ."

"This is an odd tribute," whispered Jay to Marion. "What's he getting at?"

"Oh, just the usual bit about the writer gaining immortality through his works. Shakespeare said it much better. These people could really use a copy of *Bartlett's Quotations*. I think it really means that he doesn't want to stop dressing up as Tratyn Runewind."

Jay nodded. "The author's death must have really hit him hard. Sort of a vicarious death. No more Runewind adventures."

"Don't bet on it," said Marion. "*Star Trek* ended twenty years ago, and fans are still writing new adventures for the crew of the *Enterprise*."

Clifford Morgan, with his blond hair bleached bone-white and his aquiline features, sounded less ridiculous talking "Hollywood Beowulf" than one might expect. Unlike most fen, who attended each year's con in a different costume, Morgan was always Tratyn Runewind; indeed, few people would have recognized him in nonmedieval garb. His knowledge of his alter-ego's adventures was encyclopedic, and rumor had it that during cons he was so much in character that he slept on the floor of his hotel room and ate only bread and meat, as vegetables were not part of the Celtic winter diet. Even his normal Pennsylvania accent disappeared during a con, to be replaced by his impression of Celtic speech:

a cross between Richard Burton's *Hamlet* and the poetry of Robert Burns. All of this had become so familiar to the fen, and so habitual to Morgan, that it scarcely seemed artificial anymore. Occasionally, back in the "real world," Morgan would push his maintenance cart around the hotel he worked for in Philadelphia, and mutter to himself in "Runewind," causing guests to think he was an immigrant.

He had begun his alternate identity as a skinny and backward twelve-year-old, when he first discovered the *Runewind* books. His identification with the white-maned rune warrior was strengthened in scores of D&D games, in which his fellow players allowed him to *be* Runewind. Now, ten years later, he could almost be said to commute between ancient Britain and twentieth-century America, so much of his life was invested in both places.

In some ways, he looked on Appin Dungannon as a parent: irascible, neglectful, and inadequate, perhaps, but a father-figure, nonetheless. He scanned the biographical notes he had brought with him as an aid to memory, although he scarcely needed them. Dungannon's life was as familiar to him as Runewind's.

After a few more heroics, Clifford Morgan's speech degenerated into a biography of Dungannon, gleaned from fanzines and a writers' *Who's Who*. With monotonous precision, he detailed Dungannon's education, early jobs, first publications, and so on through the Runewind books, the lawsuits, the stay at the alcohol treatment center, and the unsuccessful award nominations. The audience grew restive.

"And as a final tribute to Appin Dungannon,

we have an unscheduled performance," Morgan
announced. Ignoring Miles Perry's look of stricken
disbelief, Tratyn Runewind continued. "As you know,
the author disliked representations of his hero—"

"As *you* know!" someone yelled out.

"But since the legend has outlived its maker, we
will assume that Mr. Dungannon's objections have
been laid to rest with him, and so we will present a
short drama by the Rubicon players, entitled 'Tratyn
Runewind and the Druid Priestess.' "

Miles looked across the table at the other board
members and pantomimed the washing of his hands.
They shrugged in reply.

In the space between the audience and the speakers'
table, Clifford and several other costumed players
assembled for a whispered conference. Finally a thir-
tyish man in Robin Hood garb came to the podium to
act as narrator.

Marion recognized him as the weapons vendor
from the hucksters' room.

In ringing tones the narrator described the encounter between the Celtic hero and a Druid priestess, who, judging from her wig and costume, had
spent her winters in Egypt. After a ritual dance by
the priestess, and some divination by way of a magic
goblet filled with water from Annis' Well, a barbarian in leather and fake fur appeared, brandished
a sword at the hero, and the inevitable combat scene
took place in pantomime.

Jay Omega watched the performance with a
thoughtful attentiveness, just as he would watch the
lab's oscilloscope to detect an electrical problem.

"He's not planning to have Tratyn Runewind die, too, is he?" he asked.

"Not a chance," Marion retorted. "He'd rather shoot his mother."

After a few minutes' clattering and slashing with the reproduction (but genuine metal) swords, the barbarian gave way to the superior strength of the Rune warrior, and allowed himself to be symbolically skewered as the drama ended. He stayed dead until Runewind and the Priestess had received the initial applause, and then he and the narrator joined them to take their bows.

Miles Perry, realizing that it could have been worse, joined in the applause for the actors, and quickly turned the program over to another board member for the announcement of the scholarship winners, and for the recognition of last night's winners in the writing contest and the costume competition.

Several certificates later, he was back at the podium for the final summation, and last-minute announcements of schedule changes. "The Tratyn Runewind D&D Adventure will take place tomorrow morning as scheduled," he told the crowd. "And the DM will be none other than Rubicon's remaining guest author Jay Omega!" Jay Omega stood up for a millisecond, and Miles Perry continued, "At ten tonight, in the hotel's William Byrd Conference room, there will be a *Star Trek* wedding—this is a real wedding, folks—uniting in marriage Dave Phillips and Pamela Jarrod, as Mr. Spock and Saavik. Guests of Rubicon, particularly those in *Star Trek* costumes, are invited to attend."

Miles Perry looked nervous again. "There is one last announcement I have to make before we declare the banquet officially over. As you know, the police are investigating Appin Dungannon's death, and of course, we are all anxious to help in any way we can."

He saw that he had Lt. Ayhan's undivided attention.

"The Lieutenant in charge of the investigation has made it known to me that in his questioning of people about those with grudges against Appin Dungannon, one name is mentioned again and again. This person has written savage book reviews of the Runewind series in a number of fanzines, and in personal letters he has indicated an antipathy toward Dungannon personally, and in general he has been the most vocal critic both of the author and his work. And the Lieutenant would like to interview this individual. So . . . I thought . . . rather than mislead anybody anymore . . ."

"My god!" muttered Diefenbaker. "He's going to do it!"

"Do what?" whispered Marion.

"Will the real Chip Livingstone please stand up?"

CHAPTER 13

THANKS TO THE unscheduled murder of Appin Dungannon, Rubicon had earned its place in fannish history long before the banquet degenerated into a shouting match between rival fanzine publishers over the heretofore unexplained identity of the mysterious, fiendish Chip Livingstone, and before one desperately sincere femme fan burst into tears and subsequently severed all contact with the hobby.

Lt. Ayhan, who had simply muttered, "I love this case!" was probably the calmest person present.

The chaos had begun approximately thirty seconds after Miles Perry had asked superfan Chip Livingstone to stand and identify himself. After a moment of ionized silence, Bill Fox pushed back his chair and stood up. So did Diefenbaker. Miles Perry, who was already standing, raised his hand to indicate that he too was "standing." A wargamer from Minnesota and a Texas fanzine publisher also got to their feet.

Miles Perry explained. "Chip Livingstone has been in the hobby for only two years now, and already he has made himself prominent among the fen. He is a prolific letter-writer—of computer-generated letters—and a regular contributor to a number of fanzines. He doesn't take phone calls, but he always answers letters. And from time to time people report having met him or seen him at a con. Usually Dief, or Bill, or I will claim to have seen him at a war-gamers' convention, or in a private visit."

"I broke up with my boyfriend over him!" wailed the femme fan.

Miles Perry hesitated. "Well, he did write good letters. What happened is that the five of us created him, and we took turns writing his articles and answering his mail."

"Hold it!" yelled Richard Faber. "He was in the god-damned costume competition. I saw him!"

"Yeah! Me, too!" mumbled several wargamers.

"That was Bill," Miles Perry told them. "Remember, 'Chip' was dressed as an Imperial Storm-trooper, with full body covering and a mask you couldn't see through. You couldn't tell who it was."

"And remember," said Bill, "his character was called Sanyo the Stormtrooper, which was a tip-off. More than anything else, Chip Livingstone is a product of a Sanyo MBC-775, because all five of us own one. Think about the name! *Chip Living-Stone*."

"First a Macintosh and now a Sanyo," muttered Ayhan. "I love this case!"

"Anyway," said Miles Perry, "I thought we'd better explain that Chip Livingstone's hatred of Dungannon was just a personality trait that we invented to give him a quirk. All of us are war-gamers, so we didn't care one way or the other."

He had to raise his voice to compete with the angry mutterings of the crowd. Bernard Buchanan kept saying, "But he liked my writing. He liked my writing."

"I tell you this now, because the belief in Chip Livingstone was impeding the police investigation of Dungannon's murder. Now that you know he doesn't exist, please think harder for anyone you might know who had a reason to want to kill Appin Dungannon, and please give the police any help that you can. That's all I have to say. Good night."

No one moved. Ayhan looked skeptical. The rumblings grew louder.

Finally, above the wrangling, Bernard Buchanan's voice rang out, "Fellow fen! In the video lounge in ten minutes! There will be a memorial service to honor the memory of our lost friend—Chip Livingstone!"

"All right!" someone yelled. "To the video lounge."

Scattered applause grew into a standing ovation, and the bereaved and indignant Bernard Buchanan marched off toward the TV room with a trail of bewildered mourners in his wake.

Despite the bouquet of plastic flowers on the table at the front, the William Byrd Conference room looked not much like a chapel, and nothing at all like the bridge of the *Enterprise*, where the wedding was supposed to be taking place. The imitation wood paneling and short green drapes were more conducive to a discussion of tax shelters than to a marriage ceremony.

"In the midst of death we are in life," murmured Jay Omega, who thought it was time he said something profound.

"Don't you start!" hissed Marion. "You've done quite enough already. Besides, I was counting on you to remain sane."

"How can I be sane? I think we've fallen down the rabbit hole!" He nodded toward the lectern at the front of the William Byrd conference room, where an embarrassed-looking gentleman in the red dress uniform of a Star Fleet officer stood holding a white leather Bible. Ushers who were evidently members of the *Enterprise* engineering crew were escorting fellow shipmates and other costumed guests to the folding chairs on either side of the red-carpeted aisle.

"Romulan or Vulcan?" the ushers asked each guest.

Marion, who had been poised to say "friends of the bride," had responded to the question with an open-mouthed stare, and Jay Omega answered, "Klingon!" which got them seats in the back row of the Romulan side.

"Do you suppose their parents are here?" asked Marion.

"Why not?" asked Jay Omega. "*Your* mother once remarked that if you'd get married again, she'd be so grateful she'd come to the ceremony, even if she had to sky dive out of the Concorde."

"She didn't say anything of the kind!"

"Well, she probably *thinks* it."

Marion made a face. "Going to make an honest woman of me, then?"

"You mean stick one of those worms in your ear, like in *The Wrath of Khan*, so you'd tell the truth?"

Marion told him to stick it in his ear, and further discussion was precluded by the sound of "Amazing

Grace" played on a bagpipe. The audience turned to stare at Donnie McRory, stuffed into a homemade kilt two sizes too small, marching slowly up the aisle holding—but not playing—the bagpipe.

"Pipe her up, Scotty!" someone called out.

The music, which when one listened carefully, was actually several bagpipes, plus a few drums (the entire Strathclyde Police Pipe Band, to be exact), was coming from a cassette tape recorder on a chair by the window. Donnie McRory, who owned neither kilt nor bagpipe, was authentically Scottish, as *Star Trek*'s James Doohan was not, but as a stereotype he was remarkably disappointing. Only his Glasgow accent tallied with American expectations of the "typical" Scot.

"How do I get meself into these situations?" McRory was asking himself as he marched down the aisle. "Is it the American beer, or what?"

Having given the matter some thought, McRory decided that he got into these situations because there wasn't much else to do when you're by yourself on a tour, and also because people kept *asking* outrageous things of him. Being a reserved Briton, McRory was psychologically unprepared for the American audacity of imposing on people. He was usually so taken aback at the pushiness of their requests that he found himself complying rather than compound the embarrassment by refusing.

As the tape recorder launched into "Scotland the Brave," the bridegroom, in his blue science officer's uniform, came and stood by the lectern, accompanied by a heavyset, blond "Chekov." He gave the four-fingered Vulcan peace sign to the audience, and smiled.

"What do you think of getting married in costume?" asked Jay Omega.

Marion shrugged. "What do you call spending eight hundred dollars for a white satin gown you'll only wear once? —Was that question academic, by the way?"

"Absolutely," Jay assured her.

They turned around to watch as bridesmaids representing Nurse Chappell and Lt. Rand inched up the aisle in their black boots and the sexist Sixties costumes that passed for the "women's wear" of the twenty-third century. In their hands they carried small black gadgets decorated with white satin ribbons and baby's breath.

"Isn't that sweet?" said Marion. "They're carrying Tri-Corders."

Jay Omega leaned over for a closer look. "Tri-Corders, hell!" he muttered. "Those things are stud-finders."

"Ooh! Where can you buy one?"

"No, Trashmind! I mean a device for locating wooden beams inside the walls. Carpenters use them."

"Oh. Too bad, because it sounded—"

"Shh! Here comes the bride!"

In deference to her well-padded thighs, Pamela Jarrod wore a knee-length modification of Saavik's mini-skirted uniform, and very high boots. Her dark brown hair, augmented by a fake chignon, was swept up in accordance with regulation Star Fleet dress codes, revealing a very convincing pair of pointed ears. She carried a metal sculpture bouquet of aluminum flowers.

The reverend "Captain Kirk" extracted a typed notecard from his Bible, and summoned up a wan smile. "Dearly beloved," he said to the assembled company, "we are here to launch a life voyage of this *Enterprise* couple, David and Pamela, whose lifetime mission is to seek out strange new worlds—"

Jay Omega clutched Marion's hand, looking as if he were going to choke.

"What is it?" she whispered anxiously.

He managed to hiss back, "Is the groom going to go where no man has gone before?"

For the rest of the wedding, they had to pretend they were crying.

Donnie McRory was relieved to discover that the blue Romulan ale served at the wedding reception was in fact draft Moosehead with food coloring. The general good will of the festivities had mellowed him to the point of actually volunteering to play for the reception, but the happy Trekkies explained that he would only be needed to appear in the wedding photographs, and that they would be quite happy with their tape-recorded soundtracks from the *Star Trek* movies.

He decided that he would make a really late night of it, and then call Margaret in Glasgow just about the time she'd be getting up. She wouldn't believe a word of it, of course, but the newlyweds had promised to send him prints of the pictures. Nice lot these sky-fi people were, he thought. Odd how interested they were in Scotland. Just before the wedding, a funny old gent with a gray crew-cut had come up to him in the hall, asking if he were a member of the Scottish Archaeological Society. Fancy that. Not wanting to disappoint a culture-minded Yank, Donnie had claimed a deep personal interest in the organization. After all, he had sent them a donation of two pounds when the Lewis chessmen went on exhibit in Edinburgh, and he'd been on their mailing list ever since. The old gent seemed excited no end by Donnie's knowledge of the Scottish archaeologists; took notes about everything in a little blue book; said he'd like to drop by in the morning and talk about it.

Donnie McRory sipped his beer, wondering why Mr. Ayhan had asked so many questions about the archaeologists' fund-raising efforts. He shrugged. Probably just another potty American. They were always on about something.

Marion didn't know whether it was the bilious blue color of the "Romulan ale" or the almost palpable reek of body odor emanating from the guest in the brown leisure suit, but she was ready to call it a night. She looked around at the clumps of Trekkies and Middle Earthlings nibbling Kroger-Deli carrot cake and cheese puffs, and decided that it was all unutterably sad. She supposed that the bride and groom would go home to a one-bedroom apartment filled with tatty paperbacks, stacks of back issues of *F & SF*, and furniture from their parents' garages. The bride had happily confided that she had just graduated with a degree in history, and that she had already landed a job at Burger King which would see them through the groom's two more years as a com-

puter science major. Marion hoped that one of the
elves around the beer tap could grant wishes: this
couple was going to need a gross of them.

"Are you ready to go yet?" she asked Jay Omega.
"Don't forget that you have to figure out how to run
a dungeon between now and tomorrow morning."

He nodded. "I guess so. The first thing I need to
know is where this game is supposed to take place.
Nobody mentioned that."

"You're going to feel right at home," grinned
Marion. "It's scheduled for the high-tech room. I
think the hotel needed a couple of the other conference rooms for other groups, and since you won't
have more than fifteen people there shouldn't be any
problem . . ."

"Computer room?" Jay evinced enthusiasm. "I
think I'll drop down and check things out. I didn't
see that editor around tonight, did you? I wonder
how he's getting along with the disk . . ."

"Who cares? Joel's helping him anyway, isn't he?"

"That's right," said Jay distractedly. "Joel . . . I
think I'll just see how they're doing. Do you want to
come?"

Marion shook her head. "I'll be up in the room,
studying the scenario they gave you. Don't be too
long!" She kissed him on the cheek. "You know how
jealous I am of computers."

"I know. I think it's a glitch in your programming."

By now it was nearly midnight, and most of the
con participants had dispersed to private parties in
the guests' rooms. Lt. Ayhan had called it a night

shortly after eleven, deciding to wait for the ballistics report and the results of other inquiries before continuing his investigation in the morning. In the video lounge Bonnenberger and two other Top Secret players were planning a surprise attack on that dreaded terrorist organization, The Omaha Rotary Club, while on the television screen *Superman II* played to an audience of empty couches. Somewhere on the sixth floor, Richard Faber lay on his back, panting, and reflecting on the fact that he was no longer eligible to capture unicorns; that he had lost all hope of performing miracles as Lancelot once could; and that he was now Unfit for Minotaur Consumption. Virginity did have its mystic qualities, but he thought, as he reached for Brenda Lindenfeld, experience was handier on a day-to-day basis.

Jay Omega reached the door of the high-tech exhibit room before it occurred to him that it was nearly midnight on a Saturday, and that any con personnel in their right minds would keep the place locked. He was sure that the equipment was all on loan from various electronics firms.

He had been wondering how to go about finding Joel Schumann, and whether he should even bother, when he noticed a line of light under the closed door of the room. Trying the door knob, he found it was unlocked after all.

Joel Schumann was asleep all right, but not in his room. He was curled up in a swivel chair using his windbreaker for a pillow, while at the computer table Louis Warren peered into the TV monitor, flicking up another screenful of green letters.

Jay Omega tiptoed up to Warren's chair. "Is that

Appin Dungannon's book you're reading?" he whispered.

"Yes," the editor whispered back. "I just wanted to make sure that the manuscript's all there, and in some kind of publishable form, because when I get back to New York, my bosses will ask me that as soon as I walk in. I'll be finished soon. I didn't know how to turn this stuff off, so Joel very kindly volunteered to stay."

Jay Omega looked around the room. There was an empty table and a collection of folding chairs in readiness for the morning's D&D game. He noticed the Macintosh in its usual place beside its printer. "Did the police check out that computer?"

"The one the note was written on? Yes. Joel made them be pretty careful with the fingerprint powder, so I don't think they damaged the machine. There weren't any prints, though. I overheard one of them telling Ayhan."

"Did Joel remember who had used it?"

"About half the convention, I think. Apparently this room is very popular with wargamers. Some of them were very annoyed tonight because I wouldn't give up the IBM-PC." Louis Warren yawned. "These machines aren't too bad, I guess. I'm just afraid I'll push the wrong button and make everything disappear."

"That's not likely," smiled Jay Omega, who had had the same conversation with Marion. "Just don't agree to anything that says *delete*."

The editor still looked worried. "Do you suppose there's another disk containing part of the manuscript? Is this disk full?"

With a few taps, Jay Omega summoned up the directory. "No, it's fine," he said. "There's still about twenty percent of the disk space left. Why?"

"Well ... unless Appin Dungannon changed his methods, there's something missing."

"The book doesn't make sense?"

"No. It's all here. Once we correct the typos and his variations in name spellings, it'll be ready to go, but I was expecting to find something that isn't on this disk."

"What's missing?"

Louis Warren explained. ". . . And on every one of the eighteen Runewind books that I've edited, it has always been there. It's sort of a trademark. His own form of protest, I guess. We never let it get into the publicity releases, of course, because it wouldn't look good for the series. But I don't think he'd quit doing it, no matter how rushed he was."

Jay Omega studied the disk's directory. "It could have been erased," he conceded.

"I guess we'll never know, then." The editor shrugged.

"Oh, sure we will. Unless the guy really knew his stuff, we can probably get it back. Excuse me while I wake up Joel."

While Joel Schumann sipped his Dr. Pepper, yawned, and tried to boot up his brain, Jay Omega explained the situation to Louis Warren. "You see, when you erase a file on a disk, you don't really erase it right then. You just render that file unable to be found by the directory. So if you—"

Louis Warren smiled and nodded and smiled some more. It was gibberish; it was technical; it was

Sanskrit. In the back of his mind he wondered if the publisher would switch him over to something more restful, like Gothic romances. SF was making his head hurt.

Joel Schumann yawned again and stretched. "You mean you just want to take a look at a file that somebody erased, but the disk is okay?"

"It's the one you put in the computer for me," Louis Warren told him.

"Oh, that one. Because if it had Coke spilled on it, or a staple through it, or you'd stepped on it, there's a place out on the West Coast that'll read it for you anyhow. They charge two hundred bucks, though, and it takes a while."

"No, this is just a regular disk," said Jay Omega. "If you've got your Norton disk, it shouldn't take us very long."

Louis Warren thought that they might as well draw pentagrams on the floor and rattle chicken bones, while they were at it. None of it made much sense to him, and he was too tired to devote many brain cells to it, anyway.

Joel Schumann rooted around in a file box full of disks, pulled out the one he wanted, and shooed Louis away from the computer. "Won't take long," he remarked cheerfully.

Louis sank into the swivel chair and closed his eyes. "If you find anything, let me know." His mind settled into a happy reverie involving Jackie Collins, *Vogue*, and a word processor with keys that said CHOP and PUREE. Every now and then he could hear remarks from the sorcerer's apprentices across the room. Things like, ". . . file may be displaced by a later entry . . ." and "eight two-sector clusters . . ."

Several best sellers later, he heard the talking grow louder. "Okay, the right arrow takes you from sector one to sector two, and F8 finds the next pair in sequence."

"It'll be choppy, but it's coming."

Someone shook his arm. "Wake up, Mr. Warren. We've got something on the screen for you to look at."

The editor ambled back to the computer desk and peered at the gaggle of words in mid-screen, surrounded by various bits of technical hieroglyphics.

The ruddy Norse blonde, who was built like a human draft horse, winced a bit as Tratyn Runewind came toward her. He had only had two baths in his life: one the day he was born and one the day after he got drunk in the cow byre, but that was not the . . ."

"Hmm. Sector two is garbled. Try another pair," said Jay Omega.

Joel hit another key, and soon a new scrap of text materialized on the display monitor.

Tratyn Runewind strained at the ropes which bound him to the stakes in the floor of the mead hall.

When he had agreed to let Ole Redbeard's men tie him down spreadeagled on his stomach, he had naturally expected a romantic evening to follow, but the playful nibble at his left buttock

*was not foreplay from a burly oarsman, but an
enterprising rat who liked his meat fresh.
Runewind felt little cold noses at his ears and
toes . . .*

Joel Schumann sank back in his chair. "What is
this stuff? I've read the Tratyn Runewind books, and
they're definitely not like this!"

"Is this what you're looking for?" asked Jay
Omega.

Louis Warren nodded. "Yes, it's fairly mild com-
pared to some of the alternate last chapters I've
seen."

Jay shook his head. "I don't get it."

"Appin Dungannon hated Tratyn Runewind?"
asked Joel.

"Bingo!" said Louis. "But he had to keep writing
the novels, because they were so popular. So to vent
his frustration he would write two last chapters to
every one of his books.

"You should have seen some of the others,"
grunted the editor. "Tratyn Runewind having a bout
with dysentery during a battle, and getting stabbed
by a twelve-year-old boy; Runewind being castrated
by a Druid priestess who greatly resembled Mrs.
Dungannon. I never knew what to expect. He'd send
it in along with the manuscript, just before the last
chapter, and I'd always take it out before I sent it to
press. But that's one piece of Dungannon trivia that
nobody knew; people might get upset to know how
much he hated the series."

Joel Schumann nodded. "The fantasy people would
freak if they read this, all right."

Jay Omega gave a start. He looked at Joel and then back at the screen. "When do you suppose this was written?"

"Judging from the times on the existing directory entries, I'd say sometime Friday night. The real last chapter was written Saturday morning. Why?"

"Oh, nothing . . ." He stared at the green letters on the monitor, lost in thought. It seemed to make sense. He wondered if that was an ominous sign that he had been around the fen too long.

He was still gazing at the monitor. He had an idea. "Let's see how much more of this there is," he said to Joel.

At one-thirty in the morning, Marion was sprawled across the bed in a pile of maps and D&D manuals, fast asleep. Jay Omega smiled down at her, thinking that she looked like a vulnerable little girl when she slept. She wouldn't thank him for that observation! Despite the fact that she was a complete rabbit about math and at the mercy of almost any mechanical device, she liked to think that there were no intellectual differences between them. She seemed to think that his inability to quote Auden and the fact that Thomas Hardy put him to sleep evened the score. She didn't seem to realize that the intelligence he admired in her had nothing to do with literature. He liked the fact that she really listened when he explained something technical, and that she kept asking questions until his explanations made sense to her; he admired her versatility—they had lunch almost every day and never ran out of things to talk about, without resorting to shop talk or campus

gossip; and he was a little afraid of her perceptive-
ness: she knew things about him that he'd never
dream of telling her.

He wondered if she would guess what he was up
to now. He wasn't quite sure himself, or at least
he didn't really want to discuss it. It was just the
glimmering of an idea, and he felt it would be better
kept to himself—just in case he was wrong. How
hard could it be to run a Dungeon? Maybe he could
manage without her. Jay Omega picked up the game
scenario and studied it for a few minutes, but he
decided that it was too important for him to bluff his
way through it.

"Wake up," he said, gently shaking the bed. "You
have to teach me how to run a Dungeon, and I have a
few variations to put in."

Marion groaned. "Sorry. Your fairy godmother is
on down time. Unless you want to do an R-rated version of *Sleeping Beauty*, in which case you have a
chance of waking me up."

He shook the bed again. "Wake up, Mrs. Peel! The
game's afoot!"

CHAPTER 14

MILES PERRY WAS reflecting on how correct Einstein had been about time being relative. This con, for example, had managed to last for about twenty years within the space of one weekend. He found himself actually looking forward to the real world, in which he could manage the grocery produce section with relatively little turmoil, without having to worry about hotel damage fees, elves who lost their room keys, and famous dead people.

He had spent a weary hour the night before with Lt. Ayhan, who had questioned the entire "Chip Livingstone Consortium" right after the banquet. They had all been fingerprinted, and all had assured him that they had no access to guns, but the Lieutenant had pointed out that since his other suspects were computers and fictional characters, they were his best bet.

When Ayhan had appeared in the hotel lobby early this morning, Miles had braced himself for another round, but the Lieutenant was there, he said, responding to a phone call from Dr. Marion Farley. Miles Perry sat down and started to search the newspaper for a write-up on Dungannon.

"You through with the book section, yet?" asked Diefenbaker, sinking down in the chair beside him.

Miles Perry handed it over without a word.

"Thanks," said Dief. "I think I'm setting a new world record for lack of sleep. And I thought grad school was bad!"

"Who cornered you this time? You didn't go to the Chip Livingstone Memorial Service, did you?"

"No," said Dief. "I'd have felt like a murderer. They didn't invite me anyway. But I hear that Bernard Buchanan is trying to figure out which one of us praised his writing."

Miles grunted. "The one with the most sadistic sense of humor."

"I thought it was you!" said Dief.

"I thought it was you!" echoed Miles innocently. "So, where were you till all hours?"

"In a Far Brandonian council meeting. I can't figure out why Richard Faber wasn't there. He's been moaning about armies on his southern border all weekend."

"I think he has something else on his southern border at the moment," said Miles.

Dief grinned. "I've been waiting for Lt. Ayhan to start looking for C.D. Novibazaar. People certainly talk enough about him."

"Ah, yes, your player character in the game. Yes, that's all Ayhan needs, another imaginary suspect." He folded the paper and stood up. "Good morning, Dr. Omega!"

Jay Omega managed a groan that resembled the syllables of "good morning." He looked as if he had forgotten to shave. "I usually get more rest than this," he mumbled.

Miles Perry looked anxious. "You'll be ready for the D&D game at ten, won't you?"

Jay Omega nodded. "Yes. That's what I came to talk to you about. Is Lt. Ayhan here yet?"

"He's around somewhere, asking questions. Why?"

"Just ask him to look me up, will you? I'll be in the high-tech room."

He wandered off in the direction of the dining room, and Miles Perry went back to his newspaper. When he had any energy to spare, he would wonder what that exchange had been about.

The prospect of a celebrity Dungeon Master had lured a cross-section of con participants to the high-tech room for the exhibition D&D adventure. The computers and tech equipment had been shoved to the back to make room for the circle of participants, and onlookers were crammed into available space. A few lucky ones had latched onto wooden chairs. Of the twelve chosen to demonstrate their skill for the audience, only one had dropped out after the substitution of Omega for Dungannon as DM. Miss Megan (Beef) Wellington had withdrawn from the game, deciding that an acquaintance with the author of (shudder) *Bimbos of the Death Sun* would do nothing to help her chances of publishing her fantasy novel, the 560-page *Chronicles of Karamecia*. Three others had either overslept or left the con early, leaving eight remaining adventurers to play the game.

Most of the players had come in some sort of costume. Richard Faber had borrowed a cloak from his beloved Brenda in honor of the occasion. She had come to cheer him on from the spectators' gallery. Diefenbaker, who was a born experimenter given very few chances outside Fandom, had borrowed a feathered elf cap from Saffron; and Clifford Morgan was in full Tratyn Runewind regalia, complete with cape and broadsword. Bill Fox had on a tunic and shortsword, and the jock from the costume competition was back in his Conan costume. Bernard Buchanan wore a T-shirt stretched to the bursting point, and a button that said: KISS ME, I'M ELVISH.

"Should I wear some kind of get-up?" Jay had asked Marion.

"The cap and gown you always wear to graduation comes to mind," said Marion dryly. "No, seriously, I don't think it's necessary. The DM is basically God, and God wears anything He wants. —He looks particularly nice in jeans and a sweatshirt," she added, smiling.

A few minutes before ten, Marion, back in her Mrs. Peel jumpsuit, appeared carrying a stack of weapons charts and other data necessary for conducting the adventure. "God could use a computer for this," grumbled the Dungeon Master.

"Don't panic," said Marion. "As long as you're plausible no one will complain. If they do, turn them into a pillar of salt."

Jay Omega glanced again at the scenario, and out at the rows of spectators, seated on the floor between computer displays. Lt. Ayhan was not among them. He glanced at his watch: ten o'clock. Let the games begin.

"You realize," he said to Clifford Morgan, "that

you can't play Tratyn Runewind. He's an NPC. You'll be assigned somebody else."

Morgan nodded impatiently. His white hair was held in place by a leather thong tied around his head, and he wore a rope belt around his tunic of home-spun wool. As he eased himself to the floor in front of the Dungeon Master, he took care not to sit on his blue velvet tunic, which had been brushed spot-less, and was not the sort of garment one usually wore to loll about on a tile floor. While the other players looked like partyers anticipating a good time, Morgan managed a look of intense dedication, sug-gesting a soldier awaiting battle orders.

"Okay," said Jay Omega. "Everybody, listen up!" He turned back to Marion. "I don't have to say for-sooth or anything, do I?"

"No!" whispered Marion. "But try not to talk like Bear Bryant, either."

"Who is she?" asked one of the younger elves.

"I'm the Oracle of Delphi," Marion replied. "He consults me on close calls."

"But the DM is omnipotent," said the elf.

"Don't hassle an oracle, kid. You could end up as souvlaki."

Lt. Ayhan appeared in the doorway. "Somebody here wanted to see me?"

Jay Omega motioned for him to come over. "I asked you to sit in on this, because I think something interesting may develop."

Ayhan looked pained. "Even if it were my day off, I don't think I could find the time for *this*."

"Trust me. It's important."

"I don't play kids' games, and I definitely don't sit on floors."

Marion patted the desktop beside her. "You can come and sit beside me. I'll even explain the game to you."

Ayhan consulted his watch. "I'll consider this a coffee break." He hoisted himself up on the desk beside Marion.

"I'll have to whisper, so that we don't disturb the game, Lieutenant. What do you want to know?"

Ayhan studied the scene in front of him. "I see a bunch of kids sitting around on the floor wearing funny outfits and playing with dice. What's to know?"

"Plenty. It's a role-playing game. All the action is imaginary."

"Where's the board?"

"There isn't one. Jay has a script of the adventure, but it all takes place in the imagination."

Ayhan sighed. "Then what am I supposed to watch?"

Marion smiled. "Get into the spirit of it, lieutenant. If Jay does a good job of describing things, it can come to seem very real after a while."

"So who's Dr. Omega supposed to be?"

"He's called the Dungeon Master. He's like the Stage Manager in *Our Town*."

"Thanks for the clarification," said Ayhan, stifling a yawn.

Marion sighed. "How can I put it? He tells them where they are and what they see, and they tell him what their reactions are. For example, he could say: 'You see a stone with a gold statue sitting on it.' And then the players talk it over, and decide whether to leave the statue alone, in case it's a trap, or to risk taking it."

"Okay. Suppose they decide to pick it up."

"Then they relay that information to the Dungeon Master. And he tells them what happens next, like: you have just triggered an earthquake, or an alarm goes off, or whatever."

"What are the dice for?"

"There's a whole bunch. Four-sided, six-sided, eight-sided, ten-sided, twelve-sided, twenty-sided . . . even one-hundred-sided nowadays, or you can just throw two d10s, which we in the know call a *percentile*. Had enough?" she asked, noticing Ayhan's mystified expression. "Relax. All you need to know is that a throw of the dice—whichever dice—determines the outcome of something that depends on chance. If a rope breaks and you fall, how badly did you get hurt? In real life, it will depend on whether you fell on your head or not, whether you hit a rock or soft ground, and all the other variables. In the game, the dice take care of all of life's possibilities."

Lt. Ayhan digested this information. "So you sit on the floor and imagine an adventure, and you throw dice. —Does this sound boring to you?"

"Yes," smiled Marion. "Unless you are playing with very creative people, it can be stupefying. Young male players tend to invent adventures that are all combat, and those are especially monotonous. This one should be better than that."

"Why?"

"Because I helped to write it."

"And why am I here?" asked Ayhan.

"Command performance," Marion replied. "The Dungeon Master insisted." She had wondered about that herself, though.

The adventurers were looking up at Jay Omega with eager faces. Several of them had produced pads and pencils so that they could make notes about the things he described for future reference. It was a good idea to draw a map, too, so that when the adventure was over, the party could find its way back.

Jay Omega consulted his notes. "Okay, the adventure begins. —No, that's not right." He read the pencil notes in the margin. "We have to do something else first." What did "gen. char." and "leg" mean? His learning capacities did not function well at two A.M., which is when Marion had explained it all, and he had scribbled reminders to himself.

He tried not to look at the row of earnest players in front of him. He was rattled enough. In the audience, somebody giggled. "Gen. char"—"Generate characters!" he cried, just as the silence was becoming ominous. "First, you have to generate your characters, and then I'm going to distribute legends to some of you." Legend cards were sort of house rules; Omega held up the handprinted note cards which bore extra information about the adventure and which would augment the more usual procedures. "After that, I will explain the adventure."

Marion didn't wait for Ayhan to ask. "Generating characters. Each member of the expedition will have certain skills like strength, dexterity, intelligence, and so on. They're rolling the dice to see what their attributes are. Think of it as a gene pool."

"Suppose you get lousy marks in everything?"

"Then you start over. Better than life, huh? —And your dice scores determine who you are. If you are high in intelligence, but low in strength, you might be an elf, for example. Someone high in dexterity might choose to become a thief."

Ayhan frowned. "Thief, huh? There wouldn't be any murderers in this game, would there?"

Marion hesitated. "That's a rather philosophical question, lieutenant. All the adventurers are soldiers of fortune, and as such, they might be forced to kill in self-defense, or in order to complete their mission, or—"

"Okay! Okay!" Ayhan made the football time-out signal. "It's bad enough I have to watch this without getting commercials in metaphysics."

More than twenty minutes later, the eight players had been transformed into elf fighters, clerics, human warriors, thieves, and the other usual components of a fantasy *A-Team*. They had used imaginary gold to buy imaginary weapons, and each knew his strength and other abilities, because they had been determined by a roll of the dice.

"This is, of course, a Celtic adventure," Jay Omega told the party. "Your leader is Tratyn Runewind himself."

Scattered applause came from the audience.

"Your mission, should you decide to accept it—" Jay saw Marion frown and shake her head. Get serious, he told himself, this has to be believable. He tried again:

"The adventure is to ... er ..." He glanced at the notes on the first page of his plot outline. "Oh, yes!

You have to fight a group of Norsemen who have taken over Scotland's sacred island of Iona. That's where the Scottish kings are buried, and there's a monastery there."

"It ought to be dynamite for magic," Bill Fox remarked.

"Okay . . . You're standing on a rocky beach on the west coast of the Scottish mainland . . ."

Marion leaned over and whispered to the Lieutenant. "You probably understand this already, but he has given them their assignment, and he has just told them where they are. Now they decide how to proceed."

The commandeering of a boat to take the adventurers to Iona was relatively uneventful. In his role as omnipotent game-controller, Jay Omega gave them a little rough weather to contend with on the crossing, but nothing to really worry about.

"Now," said Marion. "Try to picture all of them on a little Scottish fishing boat, crossing the choppy sea."

Jay Omega was also trying to picture the scene. "Let's see . . ." he stammered, unnerved by the eight pairs of eyes waiting for his instructions. "It's a very gray day . . . sort of spitting rain, windy. The boat is lurching in the waves. . . ."

Marion leaned over and touched Jay's shoulder. "Now!" she hissed.

"Tratyn Runewind is seasick," Jay Omega added, trying to sound casual. "He's puking over the side."

Bernard Buchanan looked puzzled. "Tratyn Runewind is *seasick*, but—" He shrugged. Talking back to a DM could be hazardous to your health.

Jay Omega glanced at his notes for "Arrival at Iona." Marion had augmented the original adventure with a few touches of her own, for which her doctorate in folklore had proved very helpful. She sat on the Macintosh table behind the Dungeon Master's chair, trying to convey no emotion at all in her expression. Oracles, she felt, should be objective. Lt. Ayhan, looking less confused, was equally impassive. While the descriptions were being given, he had waved a dollar bill at a boy in the audience and had pantomimed drinking. The kid nodded his comprehension and took off with the money.

"As the boat comes in to the shallows of the island— I don't know how far out—" Jay turned to Marion. "Would they have to worry about rocks near the beach?"

Marion scribbled a note and handed it to him. It said: "Don't be so hesitant! In this game, the truth is whatever you say it is! Be positive!"

Jay Omega folded the note and slid it into his pocket. Mustering up his most commanding expression, the one he used for discussing grades with undergrads, he said, "As the boat nears shore, you see a beautiful black horse wading in the surf."

"The sleeping warriors!" muttered Diefenbaker, remembering yesterday's adventure. Today he was a middle-aged cleric whose specialty was magic. "Thomas the Rhymer collects black horses to give to King Arthur and his army. That horse should be magic. Catch it!"

The elf with the highest dexterity rating said to Jay Omega: "I leap over the side of the boat and I try to grab the horse's mane." He rolled the dice to determine whether probability was on his side. "Did I make it?"

Jay Omega almost said, "How should I know whether you made it or not?" but then he realized that it was up to him to decide things like that, and because he had the notes about the adventure, he knew something about the horse that the players did not. "Yes," he nodded. "You have the horse's mane, but you can't let go. It starts to swim out to sea. It is now level with the boat."

"Okay," Ayhan whispered to Marion. "That kid jumped off the boat to try to catch a horse. Now how did Dr. Omega know that he can't let go, and that the horse will swim out to sea?"

Marion looked exasperated. "Because! I told you! The Dungeon Master is like God. He can make anything happen if he wants to. In this case, he has the script, which tells him that the horse is really a demon." She grinned. "I came up with that."

Sensing the danger to their comrade, the adventurers whispered among themselves on how to effect a rescue. No one offered to dive in after him.

"I consult my magic book," said Diefenbaker quickly, holding up an imaginary volume. "Do I find Thomas the Rhymer?"

"No," said Jay Omega. "Because . . . because . . ."

"You're six hundred years too early," said Marion. "Thomas the Rhymer is twelfth century."

"So I look under Water Horses," said Diefenbaker, pretending to flip pages.

"They're using imaginary books?" said Ayhan.

"Sort of. Diefenbaker is a cleric, which means he is also a scholar, so there's a chance that he'll be able to find some information that will help with the problem. He pretends to consult the book, and if Jay feels like letting him have the answer, he will pretend to let him find it in the book."

"This sounds like the way city hall operates," grinned Ayhan. His Coke arrived just then, and he took it with a smile of thanks, and waved away the change.

Jay Omega decided to give Diefenbaker a break. "Your magic book says 'See Kelpie.'"

"Kelpie!" Mona, the female warrior, who read nothing but folklore, clutched at Diefenbaker's arm. "They're demons. They play around in the water's edge until somebody gets on their backs, and then they drown them!"

Marion nodded approvingly, pleased at finding another folklore enthusiast present.

"I am running to the side of the boat with my flask of holy water!" cried Diefenbaker. "I throw the holy water on the kelpie." He rolled the dice.

Jay Omega picked a chart at random and pretended to study it. Real Dungeon Masters actually used charts to determine probability, but Marion had said that he might as well fake it, because otherwise things would get too complicated. "Okay," he said confidently, as if the chart had settled things, "the kelpie had started to dive into deep water, but you caught him on the rump with your holy water, and he disappears. Now who's going to rescue the waterlogged elf?"

"Can't I swim?" asked the elf.

"You're unconscious."

"What about Tratyn Runewind?" asked Clifford

Morgan. "He swims, and he's stronger than all of us put together."

"Which one is he?" asked Ayhan.

"Runewind? None of them. He's what is called a non-player character. It's up to Jay to tell them what he does and says. They just imagine his presence."

"How can you have an imaginary player?" Ayhan demanded.

Marion shrugged. "They're in an imaginary boat, aren't they?"

Jay Omega tossed dice of his own. "Ah, yes. Tratyn Runewind. He tries to get to the side, but the boat lurches in the waves, and he falls and hits his head against the anchor." He braced himself for a storm of argument from the players, but there was only a stunned silence. Good, thought Jay Omega, maybe this will actually work.

Little gasps came from the adventurers as they realized that their leader had been injured so early in the game. "Roll for damage," somebody said gravely.

"I get it!" whispered Ayhan, sipping his drink. "They're checking probability to see how bad he was hurt."

"Lieutenant, you're catching on," smiled Marion.

"Sixteen," said Bill Fox.

Jay Omega glanced at Marion. "He'll be out for four hours game-time, and he's down ten hit points," he told them. Too many damage points could have fatal results—but this one, while serious, was not life-threatening.

"Am I drowning?" wailed the elf, who was still flailing in the sea near the boat.

The party looked worried. Maybe this wasn't going to be such a Monty Haul dungeon after all.

Donnie McRory tossed his clothes into his suitcase, wondering if he ought to call the British Embassy just to let them know he'd been questioned in a murder case. Probably not, he decided. The police hadn't even asked him to postpone his next booking, just to leave a list of the places he'd be staying for the rest of the tour. Still, it had been an annoying interview.

"I suppose I'll have to call Scotland Yard to verify this information," Lt. Ayhan had warned the suspect.

"Bloody hell!" moaned Donnie McRory. "Don't you Yanks know anything? New Scotland Yard—*New* Scotland Yard, mind you—only deals with crimes in London."

"Sorry," grinned Ayhan. "My investigations are more likely to involve the Salvation Army flophouse than Interpol, so I'm not up on these things."

"Yes, well, when you figure out who to call, by all means check me out. I assure you that I am no more than a name on the Scottish Archaeological Society's mailing list. And I've done my share of charity benefits in my time, but shooting a bloke in the States just to get a donation for a lot of moldy castles is not my idea of philanthropy."

"Just the same," said Ayhan, not entirely convinced, "we must stay in touch."

Donnie McRory sighed and shook his head. It was just as well that he was leaving this loony bin, before things got even more cocked up. He wondered if his agent would consider a murder charge good publicity. Probably not. The punkers would thrive on it, but as a folksinger he attracted the more sedate crowd himself. Aging Sixties types who didn't want to let go of Back to the Earth. Anyway, the whole thing was too bloody stupid. Why would anyone shoot a fantasy writer? Probably one of the Martians had gone off his head. He shouldn't be easy to spot in that crowd, then. "I wish you luck in your investigation, Mr. Ayhan," he had told the policeman at the end of the interview. "I think you should be looking for a crazy person, and it'll be like trying to find a tree in a forest."

Ayhan had only smiled. "I've got my computers working on it."

Watching the D&D game from the sidelines, Brenda Lindenfeld smiled to herself, basking in a feeling of exhilaration that she usually got only from two scoops of Swiss chocolate almond ice cream. It was an unlikely reaction to occur from staring at Richard Faber—certainly no one had previously gotten much pleasure from contemplating him, but Brenda felt that he was the answer to prayer. He was still as unattractive as ever, a dismal bed partner, and gratingly boring, but she had learned that he was majoring in computer engineering. Brenda saw the words spelled out in a string of little credit cards across her mind. Finding a computer-anything major was like winning the state lottery—and the odds were better. These microchip nerds were paid indecent amounts of money. Brenda wasn't sure just what it was they did for all this money, but then she didn't care, either. If you could manage to marry one, you were home free. No more parents to nag you about school; no more hassles to support yourself on a minimum wage job; no more worries about how to pay your long-distance phone bill. Brenda didn't think she ought to take a chance on letting this one get away. She'd better get pregnant.

During a lull in the action, Richard Faber looked over to the sidelines at his beloved, watching from among the spectators. He gave her a little wave, thinking how lucky he was to have found such a soul mate; and Brenda, thinking of a big-screen TV and the complete collection of *Star Trek* videos, smiled back.

Since Jay Omega was handling things so well on his own, Marion was taking an Oracle break, leaving Lt. Ayhan in charge of miracles. She had slipped out to the Coke machine in the hall where Joel Schumann was feeding a succession of nickels into the money slot. "Getting rid of my small change," he explained. "I think there's a hole in these jeans. How's the Professor doing?"

"Surprisingly well for a novice," said Marion. "He's very adaptable."

"Yeah, he's a nice guy," Joel conceded. "Even students like him. Are you two engaged or something?"

"Or something," Marion agreed. "We'll let you know in two years."

Joel looked puzzled. "Two years?"

"Right. That's when we both come up for tenure. If we both get it, then everything's fine, and if we both get turned down, that's okay, too. But if only one of us gets it . . ."

She might as well have been speaking Bantu to a puzzled Joel. "Yeah, well, I gotta get back to this program I'm running on the IBM in there," said Joel. "I hope it works out for you two."

Marion smiled. "That's why I keep writing journal articles."

In the high-tech room the mood among the adventurers was tense. Everyone was down at least two hit points, meaning that their chances of survival had diminished greatly, and the only thing anyone had gained thus far on the expedition was an ivory chessman they found on the beach at Iona. An hour and a half had passed, hitting them with a succession of insect swarms, rock falls, rainstorms, and other unheroic inconveniences. Diefenbaker found something else quite unusual, according to his legend card, his healing spells did not work on the elf's sprained ankle, and the woman warrior was more upset by maggots in the food supply than she had been by the rock fall.

"Things are looking pretty bad for the group," whispered Ayhan to Marion. "Imaginary maggots and all."

"Yes, Jay is giving them a run of bad luck," Marion agreed. "Sort of like Job in the Bible, isn't it?"

At a quarter to twelve some of the spectators began to wander away. Brenda Lindenfeld was signaling frantically to Richard Faber.

"Can we break for lunch?" Faber asked the Dungeon Master.

"No," said Jay Omega. "We play straight through. Until you win or die."

A few more people got up and left.

"Is it okay if I go to lunch now?" asked Lt. Ayhan, tapping the Dungeon Master on the shoulder.

"No," said Jay Omega without turning around. "You stay, too. I'll explain later."

Lt. Ayhan groaned. "Now what?"

Marion grinned at him. "How about an imaginary sandwich?"

Jay Omega ignored the looks of discomfort on the faces of the adventurers. Those who skipped breakfast for economy reasons were experiencing very real misery. The Dungeon Master consulted his game plan, and announced: "You are walking through a meadow on the way to the Iona monastery, and up on the hill, you see a stream of water."

"Do we see anyone there?" asked Bill Fox. "Weapons ready, everyone."

"No," said Jay Omega. "You don't see anything except a couple of rowan trees, rocks, and the creek."

"I say we keep walking," said Faber to the other adventurers.

Jay Omega paused for effect. "Tratyn Runewind claims to have seen something."

The adventurers looked alert, waiting for the Dungeon Master to produce a clue as to the next situation.

"We ask him what he sees," said Diefenbaker.

Jay Omega relayed the information from the non-player character Runewind, whose actions and utterances could only be conveyed through the Dungeon Master. "He says it looks like a woman washing clothes in the stream. She is dressed in green, and she is weeping. The clothes leave trails of red in the water."

"Oh, blast!" whispered the woman warrior, recognizing the description from her folklore text. "The Bean-Nighe! Has she seen us yet?"

"Wait a minute!" said Clifford Morgan. "What's a Ben-Nee-Yah?"

"They're supposed to be the ghosts of women who have died in childbirth," the folklore fiend explained. "They are always seen washing the blood-stained clothes of *those about to die . . .*"

"Why did Tratyn Runewind see her, when we didn't?" Morgan demanded.

Mona shrugged. "Maybe he's . . ." Her voice trailed away when she saw the look on Morgan's face.

Jay Omega pretended not to hear. "You see a stone tower on a hill in front of you. It seems to be in ruins."

Bonnenberger peeked through the door of the high-tech room, and saw the D&D game in progress. He had decided that watching a few minutes of D&D might be preferable to seeing *The Wrath of Khan* for the seventh time. Besides, someone might have a sandwich that was going to waste.

"Pardon," he said to a scowling Brenda Lindenfeld, who was trying to edge her way past him. "Lunch break soon?"

"Apparently not," she snapped. "Apparently he's going to keep them in there until they drop!"

Brenda's cash reserves of two dollars and twelve cents would not cover the lunch in a Chinese restaurant promised her by the unavoidably detained Richard Faber. Brenda wished he would die so that he could buy her lunch.

Bonnenberger blinked and shrugged. "Candy machine."

Brenda Lindenfeld looked at him with a loathing undisguised. *"Bon appétit!"*

The adventurers had taken a few minutes to discuss the implications of a stone tower on the horizon. Some of them felt that it might be a fort full of enemy soldiers, but others suggested that the monks might have used it as a hiding place for items that might prove useful to the expedition. Magic swords, perhaps. Jay Omega sat silently through their deliberations, offering no divine inspiration to help them out.

Finally Thrumpin the Elf decided to continue the action. "I approach the tower by myself. Do I see anything?"

"You see a partially open wooden door with weeds growing around it," said Jay Omega. "Tratyn Runewind offers to go with you."

"Hmm. That might be helpful in case of ambush. Okay, I accept his offer to go with me," said the Elf. "We walk up the hill toward the ruins, and I push the door open."

Jay Omega could have invented an ambush, or a booby-trap, but he didn't. "Nothing happens."

"I use my elf vision to look around in the darkness."

Written on the Dungeon Master's plan for the adventure was a list of all the things contained in the tower. Jay Omega noted that the Elf was in Room One, and he informed him of the contents listed for that room. "You see a door in the far wall, and a wooden chest beside it. Above the inside door is a branch of oak leaves that has been dipped in gold. The chest is an old one with a carving of mistletoe decorating the lid."

"Hey, look what I have on my legend card!" cried Bernard Buchanan, who had been injured in a pit trap near the beach, and wasn't good for much anymore. "My card says 'Treasure by the Golden Bough.' A bough is a tree branch, isn't it?"

They looked around for the folklore expert, but she had gone to the bathroom. Knowing that she could help them out of his well-planned trap, Jay Omega decided to force them into a hasty decision. "You hear a sound from outside."

The Elf thought fast. "I'm only six on strength," he said. "I tell Tratyn Runewind to open the door and look for the treasure."

"Okay," said Jay Omega. "Tratyn Runewind opens the door . . ."

"What's going on?" asked the returning woman warrior, stopping to peel a bit of toilet paper off her shoe. "What have you done?"

Bernard Buchanan told her about the golden bough legend. "So Thrumpin the Elf sent Tratyn Runewind through the door under the gold oak leaves."

Despite her status as Oracle, Marion was grinning.

"You dummies!" yelled Mona. "The golden bough

is *mistletoe*. Haven't you read Frazier? Don't you know anything?"

The chastened adventurers looked back at the Dungeon Master for a verdict. With a solemn stare, Jay Omega sprang his trap. "Opening the inner door has weakened the structure of the ruin. Rocks begin to fall."

Thrumpin gulped. "I dive after Tratyn Runewind."

"A boulder hits you as you approach the doorway. Roll for falling damages."

Ashen-faced, the Elf threw the six-sided dice a grand total of twenty times. Fellow adventurers gasped as the numbers mounted up. "Sixty-three," he said hoarsely.

"I'm sorry," Jay Omega said, forgetting his omnipotence. "You have died."

"Doesn't he get a saving throw?" asked Richard Faber.

"No."

Clifford Morgan turned as white as his hair. "What happened to Tratyn Runewind?" he whispered, plucking at the edge of his cloak.

Jay Omega met Morgan's wide-eyed stare with a look of detached interest. He almost told him the answer to his question but then he remembered to picture the scene. In order to know what happened to Tratyn Runewind, Morgan's character would have to have been present in the tower, so the Dungeon Master was not obliged to tell him. Omega deliberately prolonged the suspense a bit by pretending to consider the matter. At last he said to Morgan, "You are down the hill with the rest of the party. Are you going to go up to the tower and find out?"

"I'm dead," said the Elf wonderingly. "Should I go to lunch or what?"

"Okay, I think we ought to discuss this. It could be an ambush," said Bill Fox, ignoring the deceased Elf.

"If it was just a rock fall, it ought to be over by now," Richard Faber pointed out. "We haven't hit any signs of the enemy yet."

"The rocks killed Thrumpin, though," said Bernard Buchanan. "And what about the treasure? It should be in the chest, right?"

The Dungeon Master consulted his watch. "You have wasted three minutes," he informed them. "In a medical emergency that's a long time."

"We have to rescue Tratyn Runewind," cried Clifford Morgan. *"Now!"*

"I don't think we ought to rush into it," grumbled the Conan-jock.

"I think it's a trap," said the woman warrior.

"Four minutes," said Jay Omega ominously.

"I'm running up the hill," yelled Clifford Morgan. "I have my sword out . . ."

"Is anyone going with him?" asked Jay Omega.

"I'm staying here under the tree," said the Conan player nervously.

"Yeah," said Mona the warrior. "Me, too."

The others, with varying degrees of enthusiasm, said that they would follow Morgan up the hill.

"All right," said the Dungeon Master. "You are walking up the hill. When you are within one hundred yards of the castle, you hear screams."

"Runewind?" asked Diefenbaker.

"No. From down the hill. The tree you were

resting under was a shapechanger. It has grabbed the other two members of your party."

"We go back and rescue them," sighed Bernard Buchanan. "Don't we?"

Bill Fox looked at Diefenbaker and shrugged.

"Inside the ruin, you think you hear a faint cry for help."

"I go on up the hill," said Clifford Morgan.

"Me, too," said Richard Faber.

Diefenbaker sighed. "What *kind* of a shapechanger is it?"

CHAPTER 15

By TWELVE-THIRTY MOST of the spectators had drifted off in search of lunch. Lt. Ayhan was grumbling about missing lunch and having his time wasted, and Marion had promised to go for a hamburger to pacify him. Joel Schumann was still tinkering with a program on the PC, but he seemed to be paying more attention to the D&D game than he was to his own project.

The players—what was left of them—were suffering from combat fatigue. The shapechanger had managed to kill both Mona the woman warrior, and the Conan-jock, and Diefenbaker had been so badly hurt in the rescue attempt that he was down to one hit point, and his healing spells were used up.

A party of Norsemen had attacked the adventurers on the road to the monastery, killing Richard Faber with an arrow through the throat in the ambush, and mortally wounding Bill Fox in sword combat.

"Whew!" said Bill, when his fate had been pronounced. "The tension was getting to me!" He helped Richard Faber to his feet. "Wanna go to lunch?"

Faber looked guilty. "Maybe. I think I have to find somebody first. Do you like Chinese?"

The three remaining players looked at each other. Clifford Morgan was down to three hit points, which meant that any serious injury would kill him, and he had a slight concussion incurred when he pulled Tratyn Runewind out of the ruined fort. Bernard Buchanan's character was still limping, and still useless; as was Diefenbaker, who as a cleric could not use edged weapons, and his spells were gone. Their chances against the enemy looked bleak.

Jay Omega glanced wearily around the nearly empty room. "Tratyn Runewind says that only a fool would attempt such a mission with two wounded warriors and a cleric. He suggests that you plan your escape."

Clifford Morgan was pale and tired-looking, but his eyes flashed angrily at the suggestion. "Tratyn Runewind is more than mortal," he said. "He never retreats."

Marion stood up. "The Oracle is going out for hamburgers," she announced. "Would God like one?"

"No," said Jay Omega, who was as caught up in the game as the players.

Clifford Morgan was conferring with the remnants of his troops. "If we rely on the element of surprise, I think we may still have a chance," he told Bernard Buchanan. "We sneak into the monastery and pick off the Norsemen one at a time."

The Dungeon Master said, "You approach the monastery. It is surrounded by a white wall. There are Norse guards at the only gate. They do not see you."

"We duck behind some rocks," said Morgan. "We can go over the wall."

"I can't," said Bernard Buchanan. "I can hardly walk."

"My dexterity is practically nil," said Diefenbaker, "but if you insist, I'll give it a try."

Several more minutes passed while they described sneaking up to the wall, throwing the rope and grappling hook over the top, and while they debated on who should go first. Bernard Buchanan was to stand at the bottom to steady the rope.

"I'll go first," said Dief. "If any Norsemen come along the wall, you can defend the rope, and I couldn't. I do wish clerics could use weapons." He sighed. "All right, here goes. I start to climb the rope."

In real life, Walter Diefenbaker could no more climb a vertical rope hand over hand then he could spin straw into gold, but in D&D all things are possible, and one does not feel wounds and exertion except in one's ego.

Jay Omega rolled a die. "You get about halfway up the rope. One of the Norse scout parties spots you. They let fly with an arrow."

Diefenbaker slumped over. "That's it, isn't it?"

Jay Omega shrugged. "I'll roll and see."

The dice indicated that for someone with his limited stamina and hit points, it was definitely over. Diefenbaker got up rather stiffly. "I'll just sit over here and watch," he said, ambling over to an empty chair near the Macintosh.

"Too bad, kid," said Ayhan as he went past. "You gave it a good try."

"Thanks," whispered Diefenbaker, wiping his forehead with a handkerchief. "I'm afraid I wasn't any use, but you're right, I did try."

"The Norse scouting party is coming at you," said Jay Omega to Morgan and Buchanan.

"We run," said Clifford Morgan grimly. "We look for a place that will give us better odds in combat."

"I can't run!" wailed Bernard Buchanan. "My leg never healed!"

The Dungeon Master regarded Morgan with interest. "What do you do, Warrior?"

After a moment's hesitation, Morgan said, "Leave him. The mission takes precedence. Runewind and I run for . . . Is there a forest?"

"No. There's a cemetery, though. It has a lot of tall Celtic crosses."

Morgan nodded. "Good cover."

"What happens to me?" moaned Bernard Buchanan.

Jay Omega picked up the twenty-sided dice. "Hope for less than twenty," he advised.

Bernard Buchanan blew on the dice and sent them skittering across the floor. "Eighteen!" he said triumphantly.

"Oh, very good!" said the Dungeon Master. "That entitles you to something quick and painless. . . . They cut your throat with a dagger, and you die instantly."

Buchanan's expression suggested that this was not the sort of happy ending he had in mind. Dumping his character sheet and his legend paper into the nearest wastebasket, he headed toward the door. "This was not fun!" he announced to the room in general.

Lt. Ayhan looked thoughtfully at Jay Omega. Omega's face was pale and strained, and his body was tense. He seemed as deep into the fantasy as the kids were. Ayhan had been planning to walk out soon; he'd shot the whole morning here watching the game, and he still didn't know why. Just lately though, he'd felt a change in the atmosphere of the room, like a storm building up. Although all the other spectators had left, something told him to stay. Anyway, he had a hamburger coming. He could always stay and call it a lunch break. At the rate the players were dying, it couldn't be much longer now. He settled back and tried to picture Morgan and Runewind running from a horde of Vikings.

Jay Omega nodded to Clifford Morgan. "Over to you, sport."

Morgan licked his lips. "We're hiding behind crosses in the Celtic cemetery. It must be late by now. What time is it?"

"On Iona? Past nine in the evening."

"Good. Twilight. That means—"

"Not in Scotland. Sunset in the summertime is past eleven at night. Northern latitudes, you know. They can see you fine. There's eight of them, all carrying swords, none wounded."

"Runewind still has his talisman of charisma, doesn't he?" asked Morgan, frowning.

"Yeah, but it won't work on the Norsemen. They don't speak his language."

"Okay. He pulls his magic sword . . ."

"Three Norsemen rush the cross he's hiding behind. You can roll combat for him."

Morgan threw the dice.

"Fifty-one. It doesn't look good," said Jay Omega.

"He's magic," Morgan insisted. "He's got *mega*-hit points."

Tratyn Runewind, nearly invincible and nearly immortal, had never been in so much trouble before. Morgan was shaken, but still a believer. The Dungeon Master looked at the player's hands, trembling as they scooped up the dice. It was time.

Jay Omega said carefully, "Tratyn Runewind takes a good look at one of his opponents. The guy is carrying a very familiar-looking sword. It has carvings all the way down the blade."

Morgan gasped. "That sounds like Runewind's sword."

"It looks like Runewind's sword, too. It is the twin of his weapon, forged at the same time. This one is black, and it's called *Runeslayer*."

"We haven't heard about this before," Morgan protested.

"It was on a legend card," Omega lied. "But the person who had it is already dead."

"Tratyn Runewind attacks the Norsemen," whispered Morgan. He was beginning to sweat.

Jay Omega pointed to the percentile dice. "He got hurt the first time he tried that."

"He tries again!" shouted Morgan.

"Roll again, and see what happened." The more agitated Morgan got, the calmer the Dungeon Master became. His voice took on a tone of soothing indifference, of inevitability, as fatalistic as the Norsemen themselves.

Clifford Morgan looked at the dice as if they were cyanide capsules. His white hair was matted against his forehead with sweat, and he had kicked off his leather buskins, so that he was barefoot. As he crumpled the edge of his cloak in his fingers, Morgan kept trying to think of some amulet of protection he might have overlooked, or some bit of legend which would provide the key to Runewind's deliverance. There was none. None! Ten years of D&D games, and twenty-six Runewind books offered him no alternative to the choice before him: pick up the dice and throw.

His hands shook as he picked up the red plastic dice. He felt the Dungeon Master's stare, and wondered if it concealed amusement at his anguish. Clifford Morgan closed his eyes, and his lips moved, as he let the dice fall gently to the floor. The numbers blazing up at him were an eight and a one. Eighty-one. High damage, even for an immortal.

"That's no normal eighty-one," Jay Omega pointed out. "That's from a weapon that is the twin of his. Runewind's blade snaps from the counter blow."

"What?" screamed Morgan. "That blade was forged in the world fires by Gefion herself!"

"So was Runeslayer. And its owner is fighting at full strength—no loss of hit points. Tratyn Runewind goes down."

Morgan was breathing as hard as if he were living the adventure. "I run to cover him."

"You're too late," whispered the Dungeon Master. "The Norseman raises the hilt of Runeslayer level with his eyes and pushes it straight down into Tratyn Runewind's chest. You hear the crunch of steel against bone, and one thin wail of pain and fear. The Norseman straddles the body and grinds the sword in until it touches the dirt beneath. Blood comes out of Tratyn Runewind's mouth, and he dies."

"He doesn't die!" cried Clifford Morgan. "He's the hero of the saga. He *doesn't* die!"

"The Norseman kicks the body. Like a dog."

Morgan sprang to his feet and drew his own authentic reproduction broadsword from its velvet scabbard. "He doesn't die!" he screamed again.

Lt. Ayhan was suddenly alert. He reached for the pistol in his shoulder holster. "Calm down, kid," he ordered.

"Take it easy, Cliff!" said Diefenbaker quietly, from the sidelines. "It's only a game."

"No, it isn't," said Jay Omega, getting up off the desk and backing away. "It's for real, and for keeps. Tratyn Runewind is really and truly forever dead."

"No!" wailed Morgan, thrusting his sword at the Dungeon Master. "You're lying!"

"I'm the DM," said Jay Omega, backing toward Joel Schumann's desk. "I say he's dead."

Morgan swung the sword again, coming closer this time.

Lt. Ayhan drew his pistol. "This has gone far enough."

Morgan turned toward the sound of Ayhan's voice, but he didn't seem to understand the words. He swatted impatiently at the noise, as if it were a fly buzzing in his ear. "Leave me alone!"

"That's enough of that," said Ayhan. "Omega, I want everybody out of here."

"I'm staying," said Jay Omega. "Keep out of this, and let me talk to him."

Morgan, his sword point wobbling, looked from one to the other of them. Finally his gaze settled on Jay Omega, the murderer of his idol. He leaned forward, steadying the sword. Lt. Ayhan started for him.

Morgan's reflexes were good. He detected the movement out of the corner of his eye, and brought the blade of the broadsword down against the lieutenant's outstretched arm. It wasn't a sharp blade, but eight pounds of tempered steel impacting at full force is still a formidable weapon.

Ayhan felt the bone snap. The gun sprang from his fingers, clattering across the floor in Morgan's direction. He waved the sword menacingly to keep them back, while he bent and picked up the gun.

"He said it was an out-of-period weapon," giggled Morgan, examining the gun. "Not meant for a Rune Warrior." He fired once at Ayhan, shot the rest of the clip into the ceiling, and threw the gun into a corner.

The shoulder of Ayhan's gray suit leaked red, and he slumped to the floor. Diefenbaker, who had been sitting on a vacant desk watching the game, dived for the floor as soon as the shooting began. After a few frozen seconds in which he felt the gunshots echoing through his head, he calmed down enough to look around. Joel was gone, having managed to escape the room during the shooting. Ayhan was injured and Morgan seemed to have turned his attention to Jay

Omega; at least his back was to Diefenbaker. He had thrown the gun away. Diefenbaker looked at it, across the room, ruefully. Maybe, he reflected, he might be able to hit Morgan over the head with something.

Alas, this was not a D&D game. In real life, Diefenbaker's strength was minimal and his dexterity was nil. If he tried any heroics, he would only make a mess of it. Still, he felt he ought to do something besides cower under the desk. He looked over at Ayhan, unconscious on the floor. Dief thought he could creep over to Ayhan without attracting Morgan's attention. Then he might try to help the injured man or make a run to the door for help.

"Runewind" seemed unaware of Ayhan and Dief. It was as if he were alone with Jay Omega. "You must die by the sword," he said, advancing on the Dungeon Master. "It is fitting."

Jay Omega dodged behind Joel's desk. Picking up the Amdek 722 computer monitor from the IBM, Jay Omega kept repeating, "He's really dead, Morgan. "I'm an author and I know. If you're an author, you can make someone really dead."

He held the computer monitor, still plugged in like an umbilical cord, in front of him for a shield. "Really dead, Morgan."

"I saved him!" screamed Morgan. Tears were coursing down his face, and he lunged again at his tormenter. "He was going to die before, but I saved him!"

At that moment Marion appeared in the doorway with a McDonald's bag for the lieutenant. She saw Omega, still holding the computer monitor, dodging a sobbing youth who was flailing with a broadsword. For a stunned moment, she thought that this was part of the D&D game. It looked no more real than any of the other antics that took place at a con, but then she saw Diefenbaker kneeling over an unconscious Ayhan and trying to staunch his wound with a reddening handkerchief. "Dear God!" she murmured, dropping the bag. "JAY!"

Jay Omega did not glance in her direction. He kept watching Morgan and talking in a slow, steady voice. "Yeah, you've saved Tratyn Runewind once, Morgan, didn't you? He died on Dungannon's computer disk, and you erased it, didn't you?"

"Yes!" Morgan kept circling with the quivering sword, waiting.

"And then you saved him again when you shot Dungannon, so that he couldn't rewrite that chapter, didn't you?" The computer monitor was getting heavier in his hands. He had barely managed to evade Morgan's last thrust; if the kid hadn't been crying so hard, he'd have had him.

"Well, Morgan, you saved him twice. But three times is the charm. Your spells have run out. I've killed him for time and eternity."

Clifford Morgan packed all of his rage into one mighty thrust of the broadsword, aiming with all his strength for the Amdek monitor, dead center, intending to ram all the way through its plastic case and into the entrails behind it, just as the Norseman had gutted his beloved Runewind.

Jay Omega's muscles froze as he felt the sword splinter the screen of the monitor, but he realized that the simultaneous scream was not his own.

Through the flash and the smoke, the acrid smell, and the far-off scream that was definitely Marion, Omega heard one last dwindling cry from Clifford Morgan. He dropped the monitor, and Clifford Morgan, his hands still welded to the hilt of his broadsword, went down with it. The blade, still buried inside the monitor, flashed with little arcs of electricity.

Jay Omega kicked the plug out of the wall. "Somebody get some help," he said quietly.

Still in the doorway, Marion stood watching the scene, unable to break the spell of the shock, until she felt someone touch her arm. She jumped, trampling the lunch bag, and almost crying out, before she recognized a young police officer. His young face looked uncharacteristically grim. She saw the gun in his right hand.

"You won't need that," she murmured.

"Just what's going on in here, ma'am?" he demanded. "Where's the lieutenant?"

Marion felt tears on her cheeks. "You know *Hamlet*?" she asked him. " 'The play's the thing, wherein I'll catch the conscience of the king.' He played it by the book."

Bonnenberger, still maintaining squatter's rights to the video lounge, tried to concentrate on his paperback, despite the loud talking and general distraction from the group on the couches. That Mrs. Peel person couldn't seem to stop crying, and the guest author kept having to stop talking and hug her. Bonnenberger couldn't be bothered to find out why.

Miles Perry, looking somewhat less haggard, had put on a coat and tie in anticipation of television reporters with minicams.

Diefenbaker appeared in the doorway, looking solemn. "I just spoke with the rescue squad people. Lieutenant Ayhan is already conscious, and roaring about people trying to be TV heroes. He seems to have a broken forearm and a flesh wound, but he says he'll be out of the hospital by six, and none of the medics argued with him." He sighed. "I'm so glad. I felt quite inadequate with my little hand-kerchief. You know, at one point, I actually whispered one of my cleric's healing spells over him—in desperation!"

Marion smiled up at him through tears. "It couldn't have hurt."

"What about Morgan?" asked Jay Omega quietly.

Diefenbaker hung his head. "Oh, dear. I'd hoped you'd have heard already ... I ..." He took a deep breath, and plunged on. "They couldn't revive him. Too many volts."

Marion began to dab her tears. Then, as if she suddenly remembered something, she looked stern. "You might have told me, Jay," she said.

"I wasn't sure myself. I thought he'd killed Dungannon, but I couldn't figure out where he got the gun," said Jay Omega. "He obviously tried not to use one with me."

"It was Dungannon's," said Diefenbaker. "Lt. Ayhan's assistant said that ballistics phoned to tell him that it was a Smith & Wesson Model 1917, and when he asked the editor about it, Mr. Warren said that Dungannon always carried it around with him. It went with the cowboy hat."

"That makes sense. I figured Morgan had broken into Dungannon's room just after the costume competition fiasco, while we were still in the ballroom. He must have wanted to see the new book. How did he get in? Credit card in the lock?"

"Swiped the maid's keys." It was Simmons, the young cop. "He must have been hovering around the hotel somewhere. Morgan works for a hotel maintenance firm back in Philadelphia. He'd know his way around. As far as we can make it, he let himself in—"

"So," said Miles, catching on, "he erased the disk and swiped the gun?"

"Yeah. They found it in the tank of the toilet in his bathroom. It was a great place to hide it. I expect he saw it done in a movie once."

The Godfather, thought Bonnenberger, still half listening.

"I'm sorry he's dead," said Jay Omega. "I just wanted to rattle him enough to make him confess. I guess I got kind of—"

Diefenbaker cast a stricken look at Jay Omega, terrified that he might actually break down. "You were very fortunate to have escaped," Dief said hurriedly. "I'm thankful it was no worse than it was."

Marion reached for Jay's hand, but then drew back in a snit. "You might have been killed, you know. He could just as easily have shot you. I might have been sorrier for you then! Why didn't you trust me with your little secret? I wrote the damned Dungeon for you!"

Jay sighed. "I wasn't sure it would work. I shouldn't even have let you stay in the room. I didn't realize it was going to be so dangerous!"

Marion glared at him. "Thank *you*, Conan-the-Barbarian! Dangerous for me. One fantasy game and you suddenly start seeing yourself as the lord of the loincloth, and think you have to protect *me*?"

Jay looked sheepish. "Sorry, Marion. The old stereotypes do die hard. Look—can we get out of here? I don't want to talk anymore."

She sighed. "Oh, and you don't need me hassling you about it anymore either, right? Well, I'm sorry."

"No," he said, "I just said I don't want to *talk* anymore. I'm going up to the room now."

She hesitated. "Do you want to be alone?"

He held out his hand. "We still have a couple of hours before check-out . . ."

As they left the room, still holding hands, Jay Omega turned to Dief and Miles Perry. "We'll catch you before we leave."

When they were gone, Diefenbaker leaned back on the couch and sighed. "Well, Miles, I'm sorry you had so much chaos to contend with at Rubicon."

Miles had been thinking resignedly about returning to the produce section at the Food Lion, but Dief's remark brought on the glimmer of a smile. "Yes, but it will certainly give people something to talk about all year, won't it?"

"No doubt about that, Miles," said Dief cheerily. "Even fen who weren't here will have to claim they were."

"Of course . . ." said Miles with exuberance, "we

do have our work cut out for us next year. This will be a hard act to follow."

Diefenbaker blinked. "Oh, yes. Next year! I suppose we ought to start planning it now, shouldn't we?"

"Yes. We'll need some ideas to show the committee before they leave today and . . ."

Dief began to scribble notes and names on the back of his program. He paused with what he hoped was appropriate solemnity. "Too bad we won't have Clifford Morgan around," he said. "I'm sorry to lose such a colorful personality."

"I'm sorry Cliff didn't live to stand trial," Miles answered. "Can't you just imagine a courtroom full of ordinary people when 'Tratyn Runewind' stood up and pleaded self-defense?"

Diefenbaker nodded. "The mundane world wouldn't understand."

"I'm also glad the case got solved before Lt. Ayhan got around to asking me who wrote that threatening letter to Appin Dungannon," Miles added.

"Did you?" gasped Diefenbaker.

"Sure, but I didn't kill him," Miles hastened to append.

"No, of course, Miles. That goes without saying," Dief protested.

"I was planning to let Chip Livingstone take the credit for it in his next fanzine article. —Imagine my surprise when Dungannon ends up dead, and Chip Livingstone is a suspect."

"Well, at least Lt. Ayhan solved the case," said Diefenbaker. "And I think in police circles, a wound in the line of duty is something of a badge of honor, is it not?"

Miles Perry smiled. "Ayhan may get more out of this case than congratulations from his captain. Earlier today he was down in the lobby talking to Louis Warren about the possibility of publishing his memoirs. I think he was planning to call this investigation *The Case of the Killer Elves*."

Joseph Bonnenberger shook his head. These people weren't talking about the plot of a science fiction novel at all. They weren't even discussing their player characters in a role-playing game like Top Secret. Apparently they were talking about real life. Real life bored him. Bonnenberger stopped listening, and went back to his book.

In the 1950s, eight young men, dreaming
of literary immortality, buried a time capsule filled with
their science fiction stories. Now the capsule is being
dredged up because a few of those men
have become very famous....

SHARYN McCRUMB

ZOMBIES OF THE
GENE POOL

The sequel to the Edgar Award–winning
BIMBOS OF THE DEATH SUN

The excavation proceeds smoothly until a surprise guest
makes an appearance—a writer who supposedly died thirty
years ago. Still cynical and angry, he threatens to expose
secrets that have been hidden for years. When murder suddenly materializes, one man must separate science fact from
fiction—and unearth a killer with a story of his own to tell.

ZOMBIES OF THE GENE POOL
by Sharyn McCrumb

SHARYN McCRUMB